DERIC DREAM CHANGER

BOOK I OF THE DREAM WALKERS SERIES

D.M. FOLEY

Remember Your Roots Press

This book is dedicated to Mrs. Lunt, the best Math teacher I ever had. Thank you for taking the extra time to help me understand the things in Math that gave me "The deer in the headlights look."
P.S. Thank you for coming out to my first-ever book tour to buy my first book! Your support has been unwavering and is appreciated.

Note from the Author

For some, this book may be contro-versial, according to one of my sons. Especially in this era of gun violence. I agree it might be. We must never shy away from a subject because it makes us uncomfortable. It is in that discom-fort that we start critically thinking and asking questions. Questions may go unanswered, but at least we ask them.

This is how the concept of this book came about. During one of my many bouts of insomnia, my brain was processing a recent current event. The many questions and "What ifs?"

popped into my brain. Trying to figure out the underlying why of what occurred. Several questions led to plausible theories and more questions. I did research that led to even more questions. Could a solution to one problem cause another?

Unless we ask the questions and look into them, we may never know the answers. Aren't the lives of every human being worth looking into it, though?

So I write this note to help readers understand why I wrote this story. And in closing, I want to say, violence is never the answer. Love is. Understanding is. Asking for help is.

If you are having violent thoughts, please tell someone. Please ask for help to stop them before you hurt someone else or yourself. ~ D.M. Foley

D.M. FOLEY

CONTENTS

PART ONE

"**D**REAMS MUST BE HEEDED and accepted. For a great many of them come true." ~ Paracelsus

CHAPTER ONE

SIXTEEN IS A TOUGH age. The age at which you discover who you are. It was normally the time you think about what you want in life. For Deric, it was much more than that. From a young age, he had sensed things, known things. Things he couldn't explain and dared not talk about.

In his dreams, he saw events unfold he knew were real. How could he tell anyone that he saw things occur before they happened? Earthquakes that killed hundreds of people. Floods, hurricanes, tornadoes, and other less nat-ural events, like fires. They would think he was on drugs, or even worse, crazy.

It was horrifying waking up from these dreams knowing that they would come true and that there was noth-ing he could do to stop them from occurring. So, sleep was something he avoided, like the plague. His mom said even as a baby, he wasn't a good sleeper. The sole thing that soothed him was singing *You Are My Sunshine* to him. Deric wished he could tell her the truth. The reason he didn't sleep was that bad things happened when he did. Not always, but enough for him to fight sleep whenever he had a chance. So most nights, he received very little sleep. His mother gently nudged his shoulder.

"It's time for school, Deric."

He groggily rolled out of bed.

"I'm up."

As he got ready for school, he fought the fatigue he felt from not sleeping well. Only a couple of hours of sleep would make it a long day. He knew well that sleep would come eventually, even if he worked to fight it. A deep sleep would lead to dreams. The anxiety he felt with this knowledge was difficult to express to anyone, not even his mom, who was waiting with breakfast for him in the kitchen.

"Good morning. Did you sleep well?"

Deric grumbled audibly as he finished preparing for school. After he ate, he went out to the car to wait for his mom. He fought to keep his eyes open and stay awake on the ride to school.

Having school so early in the morning didn't help. It was hard to concentrate daily on his everyday school work with only a few moments of rest a night. In Algebra he was struggling to listen to Mrs. Lunt teach. With his eyelids getting heavy, it became impossible to stay awake.

He awakened, startled. The empty classroom bewildered him. Wondering where everyone had gone, he wandered into the hallway. As he studied the panther mascot on the wall, the realization hit him. This wasn't his school! Panic rose in his chest and his heart raced. He realized he must have fallen asleep. Feeling the dream state and trying hard to wake up, his palms got sweaty.

The footsteps behind him got louder and louder. He turned to see who was coming. The closer they got, he noticed a boy with sandy blonde hair and dark brown eyes carrying a gun walking towards him. In those eyes he saw no emotion, just laser focus on what he was doing.

As the youth got closer, staring into his eyes, Deric could read his thoughts.

I must kill them all.

Raising the gun, the bell rang, signaling the change of classes. The youngster shot. Screams rang out in the corridor. Deric turned and saw the horrific carnage.

The guy walked past him, stepping over the bodies. Looking for more to kill. A girl with braided black hair lost her balance behind the garbage can she had huddled behind. Falling to the floor right in front of the gun-toting boy. Her eyes widened as she froze in front of the shooter.

As the lad raised the gun, to take aim. Deric verbalized his thoughts.

"Stop, don't do it!"

The boy turned, looking confused at Deric. Wait, Deric thought, he heard me! That's never happened before. In that split second, the girl seized on the opportunity. She stood and ran to safety.

"Excuse me, Mr. Whitaker. What would you like me to stop doing?"

Mrs. Lunt was staring at him, waiting for a response.

Palms slipping from his face and shaking his head awake.

"Don't ask y the x was taken away, the x is an x for a reason. You should never ask y."

His classmates all muffled their snickers and chuckles. While Mrs. Lunt just frowned, his answer did not amuse her. Luckily for Deric, she wasn't one to give out detention.

"That snarkiness just earned you twenty-five bonus homework equations to answer. I suggest you try to stay awake from now on in my class."

"Yes, ma'am."

That wasn't the only factor he desired to solve. Thinking about the dream, knowing what it meant, he toiled on how to prevent the events from unfolding. Closing his eyes, he sought to remember every detail of the dream. He needed to know where it would occur. What school? Then what?

He would have to give a tip to the authorities. He wrote in his notebook everything he could call to mind. Every minor feature. The boy's hair color, eye color, what he was wearing, every little thing he could recall.

He had never stopped what was happening in a dream before. Or at least this was the only time he verbalized wanting to cease it. He always felt like a helpless observer in dreams prior.

The thought of being able to alter his visions excited him. The boy had heard him. Had reacted to him, and the girl got away. She was out of harm's way. At least in his dream. If he couldn't figure out how to stop the boy from shooting up the school, more than just the girl would perish.

CHAPTER TWO

GABRIEL WOKE UP SWEATING and shaking. Another nightmare. It was always the same one. He had been having it nightly for a month now. Rubbing his eyes and shaking his head, he couldn't understand why he kept having it.

There was no reason he should dream of shooting up a school. His school. None. Sure, he wasn't part of the popular crowd and he had suffered some bullying, but he didn't care that much about it. Then again, he cared little about anything or anyone in the last year.

His father had died suddenly of a heart attack a year ago. This was a devastating blow to his family. As the oldest, a lot of extra responsibilities fell on his shoulders.

The visions would concern him more if he had access to a gun. He didn't, though. So he told no one about them, not his mother, not even his therapist. He had been seeing Doctor Adams for the past three months.

Gabriel, his siblings, and his mother had moved to Long Beach four months ago when his mother had to sell the only home he had ever known. He hadn't made many friends in the time he had been at his new school, which was only a month. There were so many cliques in his school, he just didn't seem to fit in.

Since his father's death, he had found solace in spending an exorbitant amount of time online making friends in the cyber world. This was the reason that prompted his mother to get him into counseling. She felt he had been withdrawing too much from society.

Thinking back to the nightmare, there was one difference in this one. The boy with dark hair and blue eyes told him to stop. He wondered about the change in the dream, but also welcomed it.

In the dream, he was about to pull the trigger and shoot the girl with black hair and braids. When the other boy distracted him, she had gotten away. When this occurred in the dream, anger engulfed him, but now that he was awake, elation filled him. He didn't quite understand why the difference in the dream made him happy, but it was a kind of relief knowing he didn't kill everyone in his path. Maybe it meant therapy was working, or his depression medications were.

The girl was familiar. She was in several of his classes. Her name was Adeline. The thought of hurting her turned his stomach. She had always been nice to him. Maybe that was what made him happy, that he was unsuccessful in hurting her.

It was time for him to wake up his younger siblings, so he stumbled out of bed. His responsibility every morning was making sure his sisters got up, dressed, had breakfast, and when it was time for him to leave for school, walk them across the street to Mrs. Steven's house. That was where his sisters would stay until they got on the bus to go to school.

Gabriel's school was within walking distance, so he walked to school every day after dropping his sisters off. As he was waking his sisters up, he received a text. It was from his mom.

Don't forget to take your meds.

He left his sister's room and went to the medicine cabinet and took his pill. Then he texted his mom back.

Just did. The girls are getting up and ready.

Thanks. Love you, Gabe.

Love you too, mom.

"Maria, Kaira, it is time to get up. Let's go."

Maria pulled the covers over her head.

"I am still tired."

Gabriel grabbed the covers and yanked them onto the floor.

"Get up, Now!"

"Okay, okay."

Kaira got out of bed.

"Why do you two have to be so noisy every morning?"

"I wouldn't have to be noisy if you got up when I asked you to."

CHAPTER THREE

DERIC MOVED FROM CLASS to class the rest of the day wide awake. Focusing on the dream from earlier and figuring out where it would occur.

His teachers kept reminding him to stay on task with his schoolwork. Frustration built inside him, though. Stopping the school shooting was more important than learning about literary devices in English or World History.

Knowing from past dreams, he had very little time to figure things out. The dream would come and 24 hrs later he would hear the news of the exact event that he dreamed of.

The possibility of being able to stop horrific tragic events made him feel hopeful. Earthquakes. He knew he couldn't stop them, but maybe he could warn people of the impending danger of one. If he dreamed of one again.

Would people take his warnings seriously, though? Carefully, he would need to leave nameless tips. But how? Cell phones were easily traceable to the owner.

The bell rang, signaling the last period. Walking into his study hall, he placed his earbuds in and opened his chrome book. He was thankful none of his buddies were in there with him. The fewer distractions, the better it would be for him to find information.

He searched for high schools with panther mascots. Clearly remember-ing the panther on the wall in the hall-way of his dream. Seven high schools. That wasn't bad. After a few more min-utes, he could narrow the list down to three schools. The other four were private schools that required students to wear uniforms.

Remembering the dream, the stu-dents were all dressed differently. Their own individual styles. So narrow-ing the school he was looking for down to a public school led him to the three that were left.

Checking each school's website, he hoped that each of the school's pan-ther mascots was different. It would be the only way he could zero in on which school it was. After a few clicks on the first website, he realized he was down to two choices.

As Deric clicked on the next website, his heart raced. He thought, *what if I can't figure this out?* And then it crossed his mind. *What if I do figure this out? How am I supposed to stop this person from committing this atrocity?*

The website popped up, and he held his breath. When he saw the panther emblem, he released the breath he knew he had been holding. Relief washed over him because he was sure he had found the right school. A panther's head surrounded by a blue oval.

He wrote the address in his notebook. It was a school in California. He wanted to be 100% sure before he alerted the authorities, so he checked out the last school's website. Their mascot was definitely not it.

Now all he needed to do was contact the authorities and let them know about the suspect. This had to be done without giving his identity away. He feared being traced or tracked down. If this worked and they caught the potential shooter, then it would lead to too many questions. Questions he didn't know how to answer.

There was an old pay phone at the gas station down the road from his house on Route 165. The only question was whether it actually still worked. He would have to try it and find out. Thankfully, his mom had shown him old phones and knew how they worked.

The last bell rang, and he rushed to his locker. He switched out his books and what he needed to take home for homework. He almost forgot his algebra book, but then remembered his extra assignment. The thought of upsetting Mrs. Lunt more didn't sit well with him. She was one of his favorite teachers.

"Hey Deric, you wanna hang out after school today?"

His friend Marco was walking to the buses with him.

"I can't I have too much homework. Maybe tomorrow."

"Okay, maybe if you stayed awake in class, you wouldn't have so much homework."

Marco laughed and patted Deric on the shoulder.

Deric shook his head, chuckling, and put his earbuds in for the ride home on the bus. He hated the noise and couldn't wait to get his license so he could drive to school. His playlist of songs kept him occupied for the hour's ride home.

As he listened, he made his plan. First, he would get home, hop on his bike, and ride to the gas station. He would hopefully use the pay phone to call the police dept in the town that the school was in. He was optimistic they would listen. Then he would call the FBI, just to make sure they took the information contemplatively.

The bus stopped in front of his house, and he stepped down onto the pavement. Thankfully, no one was home. His parents were still at work, and so were his brothers. He let himself in the door with his key and his dog, Lexie, greeted him, wagging her tail in excitement. Ruffling her fur as he greeted her back, he then let her outside to do her business. After letting the dog back in, he grabbed the paper with the numbers and information and headed to the gas station on his bike.

CHAPTER FOUR

GABRIEL WALKED HIS SISTERS across the street to Mrs. Steven's house, then headed towards his school. It was only a couple of blocks from his house. His blue backpack was heavy against his back. The number of books he carried was enormous since he never felt he had enough time to make it to his locker between classes. He kept every single textbook with him throughout the day. As he walked past the park that was between his house and the school, he absentmindedly saw people running, walking, and jogging along the paths.

He looked at his watch. The time told him he was running early, so he veered into the park. He enjoyed walking along the paths and walked to the edge of the pond in the center of the park. There were a few flat rocks on the ground, and he picked one up and skipped it across the pond. Smiling, he remembered how his father had taught him how to skip rocks on one of their many fishing trips.

The memories of his father were difficult. He swallowed hard to keep the lump from building in his throat. The corners of his eyes stung with the buildup of tears that were threatening to spill out. He missed his father so much. Being the man of the house was heavy and stressful. He hoped his dad would be proud of him. If his dad could even see him. Gabriel didn't even know whether he believed in god or heaven.

If there really was a god, why would he take his father away from his family? He couldn't reconcile these questions with what his parents had taught him his entire life: that god was a loving father. *If he was loving, why would he inflict pain on his children?* For Gabriel, it was easier for him to think that god didn't exist and that there was nothing after death.

He shook his head, trying to clear his thoughts, and then looked at his watch again. Now he was cutting it close. He might even be late for school. Breaking into a small trot, he made it to school just in time. He walked into homeroom and sat down in front of Adeline. She smiled at him and he smiled back.

Gabriel went through his day like any other day. He kept to himself, did his school work, and took part when teachers asked questions. During lunch, he purchased hot lunch and then sat down at a table with other students that mostly kept to themselves. There was no banter among them like at the other tables. The entire table jumped when a cup of jello splattered in the middle of the table. Other tables of students were laughing and pointing at them.

It was Gabriel who got up and found paper towels to clean up the mess. He handed a paper towel to one of the other kids sitting at his table. She had been wearing a white t-shirt and some of the red jello had splattered across the front of it. He could see the tears welling up in her eyes.

"My mom is going to kill me."

"Maybe it will come out in the wash."

"I hope so. We can't afford to buy new clothes all the time. This was a hand-me-down as it is."

"I am sorry."

"Not your fault. It's the jerks who think stuff like this is harmless and funny."

"I know. It just gets me so mad that people don't think about others' situations. By the way, my name is Gabriel, but you can call me Gabe."

"My name is Mindy. Thanks for your help, Gabe."

As he finished cleaning the mess he didn't make, the bell to signal lunch was over rang. Gabriel looked at his own lunch. He had only eaten a couple of bites of it. The anger inside him boiled. His mom worked hard to provide for him and his sisters. Wasting food equated to wasting money, and it upset him. His mom made too much money to qualify them for free lunch, but they lived paycheck to paycheck. He assumed most of his peers didn't understand what this was like. However, after speaking with Mindy, he was sure she did.

For the rest of the school day, it filled his thoughts with the entitled attitude of most of his peers. He overheard conversations about how kids manipulated their parents to buy them what they wanted. Not that they needed the items, it was just that they wanted them.

Gabriel didn't understand this. If he wanted the latest video game or console, he had to earn the money. This he did by mowing lawns, raking leaves, and doing other odd jobs for his neighbors. The more he thought of his peer's entitled attitudes, the angrier he got.

The strong feeling surprised him. He hadn't really felt any emotion heavily since his father died. The last bell rang, and he was glad to be leaving school. The agitation he was feeling was getting overwhelming and confused him all at once.

As soon as he stepped outside, he felt a slight release of the anger he had been feeling. Hastily, he walked toward his home. As he reached the park, he detoured toward the pond again and skipped rocks. The tension in his body dissipated. He found a tree to sit under and pulled out his history homework. Sitting in the fresh air helped him to concentrate, and he finished his work within an hour. He felt much calmer than he had when he first left school.

He finished walking home and arrived fifteen minutes before his sisters were to be dropped off by the bus. Sitting on the front steps, he waited for Maria and Kaira to get home. They were twins and were only nine years old. Losing their dad had been rough on them, too. That's why Gabriel did his best to help take care of them. When he saw his sisters getting off the bus, he noticed Maria was walking with her head down. Kaira looked upset and cradled her arm around her sister.

Gabriel felt the agitation returning within himself as he walked towards his sisters.

"What's wrong?"

Maria's head snapped up, and she shirked her sister's arm off while elbowing her.

"Nothing. Everything is fine. Right Kaira?"

Kaira looked at Gabriel and then at Maria. Maria's eyes were wide, sending her a silent message to agree with her.

"Yeah, nothing."

Gabriel didn't believe his sisters, but he knew pressing them any further would get him nowhere. There were no physical signs of anything being wrong, but he sensed there was. His agitation grew. How could he be the man of the house and protect his sisters if they weren't honest with him? As they all entered the house, the girls ran to their room and closed the door.

"Don't forget to do your homework!"

Gabriel entered the kitchen and turned the oven to preheat. Thanks to his mom's Sunday meal prepping, all Gabriel had to do for dinner was warm it in the oven. It was done by the time she got home.

When his mom arrived, her eyes had dark circles under them and she rubbed the back of her neck. Gabriel could see the exhaustion in the way she moved to put her work bag away. His sisters came running out of their room when they heard their mother. They gave her a big hug, and she returned the affection back.

"How was school?"

Gabriel was the first to answer.

"It was okay."

Maria and Kaira exchanged a look among themselves. Gabriel caught it, but he didn't think his mother did. They replied in unison.

"Fine."

Gabriel eyed his sisters. He knew they were hiding something, and it made him angry they were keeping it from him and their mother. They all sat down to dinner and ate quietly.

His mother seemed extra tired tonight, and he caught her staring out the window on more than one occasion. He could tell she was missing his father.

"How was your day, mom?"

"Busy as usual. Thank you for asking Gabe. That used to be the first thing your dad would ask me when I got home from work."

It was both of his sisters' turns to do the dishes and clean up from dinner, so as they started, he headed to his room. In no time, he immersed himself in his online games. He chatted with his friends and answered DMs from other players. It was a typical night for him. He finally got off the computer around eleven o'clock. When his head hit the pillow, he was fast asleep within minutes.

CHAPTER FIVE

THE BICYCLE RIDE TO the gas station seemed to take forever, even though it was only a mile down the road. By the time Deric arrived, his stomach was in knots. He didn't know what he was going to say when he made the phone calls. His hands shook as he picked up the receiver and put it to his ear. Cradling it between his ear and his shoulder, he reached into his pocket for some change. He didn't know how much he would need to call California.

When he heard the dial tone, he punched the number of the police department. As soon as the person on the other end picked up, Deric froze.

"Hello, Long Beach Police Department, Natasha Fields speaking. How may I direct your call?"

Deric took in a deep breath and then released it, calming his nerves.

"Hi, um, I would like to report an incident involving a suspicious person. I believe he is going to commit a school shooting tomorrow."

"Okay, sir, what is your name? What is the name of the suspect?"

Deric ran his free hand through his hair. How was he going to explain this?

"Um, I would rather not give my name, ma'am. Can I just do this anonymously?"

"Well, son, if you want us to take you seriously, we need a name."

"Please, I really don't want to give my name. Everyone is always telling us, kids, if we see something, to say something. Here I am trying to say something, and you are making it more complicated."

"Young man, we want to take you earnestly. What you are saying is very concerning. If it is credible, then we can do something about it."

"Ma'am, with all due respect, have you heard the phrase snitches get stitches?"

"Son, of course, I have heard it. We deal with gang violence daily. Okay, give me the information and we will see what we can do. I can't promise you we will do anything."

"Ma'am, if you don't take what I am about to say sincerely, children will die. A boy about sixteen years old with sandy blonde hair and dark brown eyes wearing a yellow t-shirt and black pants will bring a gun to school tomorrow to shoot up The Long Beach High School. Oh, and he will have a black backpack on."

"That's pretty specific. How do you know what he looks like and what he will wear? What is this boy's name?"

"Ma'am, I just know, that's all. I can't tell you how I know. I don't know his name. Please, just have the police at the high school tomorrow morning to stop him."

Deric hung up the phone. He hoped they took his warning seriously, but he was so afraid they wouldn't. Next, he dialed the California FBI office number. That call went the same way. When he finished, all he could do was go home and wait. He wouldn't know until the next day whether he was successful.

His legs ached from the bike ride home and when he walked through the door to his home, he went into the living room and flopped onto the couch.

Mrs. Whitaker walked into the house, tired from working. She knew Deric was home because the door had been unlocked. The quiet was unusual, though. Normally, she could hear him playing video games in his room. She peeked into his room and when she didn't find him in there, her concern rose in her chest. Quickly, she walked through the kitchen to the living room. Letting out a sigh of relief, she saw Deric was fast asleep on the couch.

When she walked over to him, she lightly placed her hand on his forehead. It felt normal. He stirred a bit but didn't wake up. She knew he didn't sleep well most nights, so she left him.

Knowing he wasn't running a fever made her relax as well.

In the kitchen, she prepared dinner for her family. Her husband and her other two sons would be home from work soon. She tried to have a sit-down dinner with her family at least once a week. Their schedules didn't always make it possible.

Mrs. Whitaker was a collections secretary in a local law office. Most days she was home by 5:30 pm, although some days she had to work later. Sometimes she had to fill in for the receptionist when she took a day off. When that occurred, it put her behind in her own work, so she made up for it by working late the other days to catch up.

Mr. Whitaker worked on the Fishers Island Ferry as a captain. His shifts varied from day to day. Some days he worked the early shift and other days he worked the late shift. This day he was working a charter and he would be home by 6:00 pm. Deric's brothers, George and Thomas, worked as plumbers for their Uncle Mike. As long as there were no emergency calls, they would walk through the door at any moment. Mrs. Whitaker heard George and Thomas come in the front door, conversing about their day.

"Please lower your voices. Your brother is asleep on the couch. I want him to get some sleep."

George rolled his eyes at Thomas.

"Aw, little baby Deric is having a nappy nap."

Thomas laughed out loud and punched his older brother in the arm.

"Yeah, we must not wakey the precious baby."

Their mother turned to them both with her brows furrowed and her mouth forming a scowl. George elbowed Thomas when he caught the look their mom was giving them.

"Alright, alright, we will be quiet. We were just kidding, mom. You know we understand Deric doesn't sleep well."

Mrs. Whitaker unfolded her arms and softened the features on her face. She adored all three of her boys. They knew it too.

"Don't worry, I am awake."

They all turned to see Deric in the doorway between the kitchen and the living room. Mrs. Whitaker frowned again and the older boys just shrugged their shoulders.

"I am sorry. I hope your brothers and I didn't wake you up. Are you feeling alright?"

"No, you didn't wake me up and yes, I am feeling okay. What's for dinner?"

"Shepherds' pie. Your father should be home soon. Can you boys get your chores done before he does?"

In almost perfect unison, they chorused.

"Yum. Sure thing."

Deric was glad to be busy with his chores. They kept his mind off the impending tragedy that he hoped he had stopped. He would find out for sure tomorrow. They filled the rest of the evening with a family dinner and a movie. It was good to sit and spend time surrounded by those he loved and who loved him back. It helped calm his nerves.

CHAPTER SIX

NATASHA FIELDS HEARD THE silence on the other end of the line when Deric hung up. She didn't know whether to take the information he provided seriously. As she contemplated if she should pass the information on to her supervisor, she replayed what Deric said over in her mind. He was so polite and there was a frightening edge to his voice. This made her decide to call her supervisor over.

"Hey Smitty, I had a really wild call just now. I think the information is credible."

Her supervisor, Sergeant Smith, came over to Natasha's desk.

"Yeah, what's it about?"

"A school shooting."

Smitty's body went stiff and the hair on the back of his neck stood up. That was any law enforcement officer's worst fear. In the last two decades, school shootings had become somewhat commonplace. They struggled to find the exact cause. Many politicians claimed it was easy to access guns, however even with stricter gun laws, they still occurred.

"What did the caller state?"

Natasha briefed Smitty on the phone call in great detail. She also added how polite the caller was and the sound of fear in his voice that made her believe in her gut he was telling the truth. Smitty agreed there was no harm in beefing up the police presence at the high school in the morning. He went back to his desk and called the school superintendent to apprise him of the situation. As he hung up with the superintendent, his phone rang.

"Sergeant Smith, The Long Beach Police Department, who may I ask is calling?"

"Sergeant Smith, this is Special Agent Nunez with the FBI. There is a potential school shooter that will be at your local high school tomorrow according to a tip we received. We deemed it semi credible and in honesty, we would like to err on the side of caution than completely discount it."

"They called us as well. Let's compare notes. I have already added extra security at the high school tomorrow and

I just got off the phone with the super-intendent of schools. They are aware of the threat and our plan."

The two men compared notes. When they realized the caller had stated the same thing verbatim, they deemed it even more credible. Special Agent Nunez let Smitty know he would be at the department first thing in the morning to monitor the situation.

In the morning, Sergeant Smith assembled a team of officers to be visible at the school. Some wore undercover clothes. All wore their bulletproof vests. They had decided they would unload the buses one by one to make sure they could check each student as they got off the bus, and they would search their backpacks. Each entrance had an officer posted to check the walkers.

Each of the officers was on edge. They didn't want to make the students anxious, however; they knew what they were doing was what needed to be done to keep them all safe. Sergeant Smith made sure everyone was in place and knew what the plan was. They all hoped this was not the real deal.

CHAPTER SEVEN

THE ALARM ON DERIC'S phone went off and he hit snooze. He knew he could hit it three times and not be late for school. Much to his surprise, he had slept well. Even more astonishing was he had no dreams or nightmares. After his third alarm went off, he got up and got ready for school. He was still anxious about the possibility that they had ignored his warnings. The thought of innocent people dying made his stomach roil.

Deric choked down a waffle and washed it down with chocolate milk before his mom was ready to go. This didn't settle his belly. She usually dropped him off on her way to work so he could get an extra hour of sleep.

"Deric, I will meet you out in the car."

"Okay mom, I just need to brush my teeth."

His mom waited patiently for him to come out to the car. Within minutes, Deric was getting into the passenger seat. As he got in, he synced his phone to the Bluetooth in the car so he could listen to his playlist. Mrs. Whitaker smiled. She enjoyed these moments with her youngest son. She especially enjoyed the diversity in her son's music taste. They often sang along to the songs being played. It never surprised Deric that his mom knew the lyrics as well. He knew she enjoyed the music of all different genres as he did.

The school day dragged on and with each passing second, Deric grew more anxious. It was a little after 10 am when he felt the phone in his pocket vibrate. He knew it meant he had a text notification. Simultaneously, Mrs. Lunt's phone dinged.

"I apologize. I must have forgotten to silence my phone this morning."

As she picked it up to set it to silent, the students in her class took the opportunity to look at their own phones, including Deric.

It read: *Breaking News. A high school in California is on lockdown following the arrest of a student who was in possession of multiple weapons.*

Mrs. Lunt skimmed the text herself and then put her phone away. As she did, she caught several of her students staring at their own phones. Knowing she had lost their focus, she helped her students deal with the news brief.

"So, let's chat, shall we? I see many of you read the same text I did. Or at least I assume you did. So how do you feel about it?"

The students fidgeted in their seats and looked back and forth at each other. It seemed no one knew what to say. Then one girl spoke up.

"I am glad they have hurt no one, and they caught the person before they did any damage. I wish that could happen all the time."

Several students nodded their heads in agreement. Mrs. Lunt nodded her head.

"Yes, it appears even though it's scary thinking about the intent of this person, it is a colossal relief that they stopped a tragedy from occurring."

Finally, Deric came out of his daze. It worked! It really worked. He stopped the school shooting from happening. He let out a sigh of relief. It was louder than he expected and everyone was looking at him.

"I am just curious to find out how they caught the student."

Deric saved himself by saying what was on everyone's mind. The bell rang, and they carried on throughout the rest of their day. He couldn't wait to get home and watch the news. The need to know who the suspect was and how they caught him filled his thoughts. More importantly, he wanted to know if they would announce there was an anonymous tip.

The last bell rang, and he gathered his things and boarded the bus to go home. It was grueling waiting to watch the five o'clock news. Tonight was a late night for his parents and brothers. That meant a fend-for-himself night. In the freezer, he found chicken nuggets and french fries. He took out the baking sheets to cook them on, preheated the oven, and prepped the nuggets and fries.

When the news came on, the apprehension of the potential school shooter was the lead story. They didn't name the suspect because he was a juvenile. Long Beach police apprehended the suspect before he entered the building. The police had received an anonymous tip that pointed them toward the student they had in custody. They had put the school on lockdown as a precaution to make sure there were no accomplices.

Wow, they took him seriously. In doing so, he prevented a tragedy. He was thankful they had believed him.

CHAPTER EIGHT

GABRIEL SLEPT WELL. HIS mother was at work by the time he got up. The morning went as usual, except Maria gave him a hard time getting up.

"Come on, Maria, you need to get up. You will make us all late for school."

"I don't want to go to school."

"Are you sick?"

"No."

"Then you know mom's rules. Go to school. You can't just stay home because you want to. Trust me, there are some days I would love to stay home as well. But, I can't. So get up, now."

Maria's slowness in getting ready for school irritated Gabriel. Finally, they were ready. Gabriel was about to usher them out the door when he received a text. It was his mom reminding him not to forget his medication. She was sorry she was late with the text. It annoyed him he had forgotten on his own. He grumbled to himself as he went to the medicine cabinet to take it.

When he had swallowed it, he texted his mother back that he had indeed taken the pill. Then he gently prodded his sisters out the door and across the street. After his sisters were inside the neighbor's house, he turned to go down the steps.

His phone dinged, notifying him he had another text message as he walked down the steps of Mrs.

Steven's house. He read it and prompt-
ly crossed the street and went back
inside his house. Under the sink in the
kitchen, he found his dad's old toolbox.
Within the toolbox, he found a hammer. He gripped the hammer tightly
and walked to his room. It took him a
few minutes to accomplish the task at
hand. When he was done, he returned
the hammer and left the house.

The next stop he made was the
park. Instead of heading for the pond,
though, he went to the edge where
there was a clump of trees with low
bushes. He bent down and opened the
black backpack. The contents were all
there, just as promised. He zipped it
closed and headed to school with it on
his back.

As he approached the school, he
could see the buses were letting students off one by one, instead of all at

once. This scene did not bother him. It changed his plan. The backpack slid off his back as he set it down on the sidewalk. Sergeant Smith saw him and radioed to his team he had the potential suspect in his sights. They stopped unloading the buses, told them to shelter in place, and headed toward Gabriel with guns drawn.

He focused on putting the magazine inside the gun. He wasn't aware of the police, who had been moving in place to apprehend him. As he stood up with the loaded gun, police officers surrounded him. Their guns were all drawn and pointed at him. He didn't flinch. Sergeant Smith took point with the situation.

"Son, drop your weapon and no one will get hurt."

Gabriel stood there, frozen. His face showed no emotion. Sergeant Smith tried once more.

"Drop your weapon."

There was something about the look in Gabriel's eyes. Sergeant Smith recognized that look. It was familiar to him. He had seen it in pictures and mugshots of previous mass shooters. It was a haunting look, devoid of emotion. He made a split-second decision to use his taser to subdue the suspect. It hit the target and made him writhe on the ground in pain. The gun was out of Gabriel's hand and the police rushed to handcuff him.

Gabriel felt the shock of the taser. The pain seared through every one of his cells. It became apparent immediately to him he was on the ground and he had urinated on himself. His chest was tight, and he felt as if he couldn't move a muscle. He just couldn't re-member how he got here. Then there were police officers handcuffing him and yelling orders at him to remain silent. He was so confused. He saw a gun on the ground and a black back-pack. Neither belonged to him. *Was he dreaming his recurring night-mare again? If he was, this version was different.*

This felt real, though. Too real. Gabriel shook with fear. *What had he done?* He couldn't remember any-thing. Two police officers helped him to his feet in handcuffs and walked him to a police cruiser. As he sat in the back of the car, he shook his head, trying to remember what had led him to where he was currently sitting.

He remembered waking up and get-ting his sisters ready for school and bringing them across the street. The rest of the morning was a mystery. Try as he might, he could not remember walking to school. As he leaned his head against the window of the police cruiser, he watched as his fellow students were let into the school one by one. Many looked back at him with fear in their eyes. He didn't see any ambulances, so he must have hurt no one. There Adeline and Mindy were. They both looked at him with confusion and sadness.

A police officer entered the driver's side of the cruiser and started the engine. They headed to the police station. Gabriel was terrified of what was going to happen to him. *How would his mom react? Who would help his mom with his sisters?*

CHAPTER NINE

Mrs. Ingles recognized the school phone number on her cell phone and answered it. Hoping Gabriel was okay. She had received a breaking news alert stating there was a potential shooter at his school. While it relieved her that the suspect was in custody, her stomach kept stirring because Gabriel had returned none of the texts she had sent asking if he was okay.

"Hello?"

"Mrs. Ingles?"

"Yes, speaking."

"This is Mr. Muldoon over at Long Beach High School. I am not sure if you are aware we had a situation this morning that resulted in a lockdown and an arrest."

"Yes, I am aware. It has been on the news. But, they have reported that there were no injuries. So I don't know why you are calling me."

"I am calling to inform you that your son, Gabriel, is in custody. The police have taken him down to the police station for questioning."

Mrs. Ingles felt faint. The room spun around her. Her breathing became rapid and her heart pounded in her chest.

"Gabe? My Gabe? There must be some kind of mistake. We don't even own any weapons."

"I am sorry, Mrs. Ingles. The police apprehended him with the gun in his hands. If I were you, I would contact a lawyer and then head down to the station yourself."

"Thank you, Mr. Muldoon."

When she hung up, it was hard to breathe. She informed her boss that she had a family emergency and left. On the way to the police station, she called Mrs. Steven and asked if she could get the girls off the bus. Mrs. Steven was more than happy to oblige and wasn't nosey about why Gabriel couldn't do it. She figured he had picked up a side job to make some extra money, as he sometimes did.

The drive to the police station seemed to take forever. Mrs. Ingles sat in her car to gain her composure before entering. The thought of Gabriel going to jail frightened her. When she felt she could stand and walk into the police station, she got out of her car. She walked through the doors and went up to the window. There was a woman officer sitting behind the plexiglass.

"Can I help you?"

"Yes, my son, Gabriel Ingles, is being held here. They apprehended him at Long Beach High School."

"Oh. Let me let the sergeant know you are here. Have you hired an attorney yet?"

"No ma'am, I do not know who to even hire. Does he need one?"

"They arrested him for having a gun. Loaded and drawn. On school property. I would get an attorney. Here is a list of defense attorneys."

"Okay, thank you. Can I see my son?"

"One moment, Ma'am, I will get the sergeant."

The officer walked through a door and returned with Sergeant Smith, who let Mrs. Ingles back into the hallway leading to the interrogation room where Gabriel was being held in. He talked as they walked.

"Mrs. Ingles, Officer Davis tells me you don't have an attorney yet. Would you like one appointed?"

"I do not know. I am a widower, and I don't have a lot of money. Gabriel has never been in trouble in his life. He is a good boy."

"I will call to have one appointed. I would rather not question your son until there is an attorney present. And that means you can't see him either until they appoint him one. I am sorry."

Mrs. Ingles covered her face with her hands and sobbed. Sergeant Smith led her into his office. Then he called the county defense attorney. He felt for the woman sitting in his office. The principal at the school had given him background information on Gabriel. He was a good kid. Quiet and stayed out of trouble. He had lost his father a year prior.

"Mrs. Ingles, can I ask you a few questions about Gabriel?"

"Of course, I have nothing to hide."

"Has he ever been in trouble before?"

"No, never. He works for the neighbors doing side jobs to make extra money. He takes care of his sisters every day after school and before school."

"That's a lot of responsibility for a sixteen-year-old. Did he resent it?"

"No, he didn't seem to. Do you think that made him do this?"

"I don't know why he did this, ma'am. That's why I am asking these questions. What did he spend the money that he earned on?"

"Mainly video games. Sometimes he would treat us out to dinner. Or he would buy his sisters something they really wanted."

"Could he have bought the gun with that money?"

"I don't think so. He went nowhere without me. Except for school and his odd jobs."

"Are you sure?"

"Yes."

There was a knock at the door and Sergent Smith opened it to see a man in a grey pin-striped suit.

"Attorney Whitty, let me show you to your client. Mrs. Ingles, please wait here until I come to get you."

The two men left and walked down the hallway. They entered the interrogation room, where Gabriel was waiting. They'd cuffed his hands in front of him and he was holding his head in them. His eyes were red from crying.

"Gabriel, I am Attorney Whitty. They have appointed me to be your defense attorney. Can you and I have a private conversation before the police ask you questions?"

"I guess."

Sergeant Smith left the room. Another police officer came up to him.

"Sir, we have the search warrant for the house. When do you want us to execute it?"

"Well, come with me, and let's present Mrs. Ingles with the warrant. She is in my office. "

Sergeant Smith presented Mrs. Ingles with the warrant. He asked if she would like to be present when they searched the house. She told them no and handed them the keys. All she wanted was to see her son.

Sergeant Smith's phone rang. It was attorney Whitty letting him know they were ready for questioning.

"Mrs. Ingles, I am going to allow you to sit in on the questioning as long as you don't get emotional or interfere with our investigation. Gabriel is a minor. But, I want you to know his case is highly likely to be transferred to adult court based on the severity of the charges."

"Okay."

Mrs. Ingles didn't know what else to say. She just wanted to see her son. They walked together into the interrogation room. When Gabriel saw his mom, he burst into sobs.

"I'm sorry, mom."

Mrs. Ingles hugged her son.

"It's okay Gabe. Tell the truth, tell them everything."

"I will, mom."

Sergeant Smith sat across the table from Gabriel, who had his lawyer sitting on one side of him and his mother on the other. Then Agent Nunez entered and sat down next to sergeant Smith.

CHAPTER TEN

GABRIEL DIDN'T UNDERSTAND WHAT was happening to him. He knew he was under arrest. They were charging him with possession of a firearm on school grounds. They said he was planning on shooting up the school. He had no memory of obtaining the gun or wanting to hurt anyone. He remembered the nightmares he had. They scared him; they hadn't excited him or anything. He didn't want to hurt anyone.

The men sitting across from him seemed stern. Not angry, but they definitely meant business. He waited for them to question him. His attorney had advised him to tell the truth. That is what he intended to do. He promised his mom he would. Just seeing her here made him feel horrible. She didn't deserve to be going through this.

"Gabriel, my name is Sergeant Smith, and this is Special Agent Nunez with the FBI. We want to understand why you wanted to shoot up your school. Can you answer some questions for us?"

"Yes, sir. I will do my best."

"Why did you want to shoot up your school?"

"I didn't."

"We know you didn't accomplish your goal because we stopped you. But why would you bring a loaded gun to school?"

Gabriel looked at his attorney, who nodded to him to answer the question.

"I don't know. I don't remember."

"What do you mean you don't know? How can you not know why you brought a gun to school?"

"Sir, I am telling you the truth. All I remember is dropping my sisters off at the neighbor's house like I do every morning. The next thing I know, I am on the ground in excruciating pain and peeing myself. I remember nothing in between."

Sergeant Smith and Agent Nunez looked at each other. It horrified Mrs. Ingles with what her son had recounted. She hadn't realized that the police used a taser on him. It was Agent Nunez who spoke next.

"Son, you realize they will probably try you as an adult and you are facing life in prison?"

"Sir, yes. My attorney has advised me of that. It doesn't change what I said. I seriously remember nothing."

"Who was your friend that tipped us off? He knew everything about you, except he didn't give us your name. He even knew what you would be wearing."

This question was shocking to Gabriel. He had no friends. At least none at school. All his friends were online, and he never discussed things like what he was going to wear to school with them.

"Sir, I don't know. I don't have any friends except for ones online."

"Did you tell them of your plans?"

"I didn't have any plans. I didn't want to shoot up my school or hurt anyone!"

"Where did you get the gun?"

"I don't know! I have never seen it before in my life until I was on the ground from being tased!"

Gabriel had lied. He had seen the gun and the backpack before in his night-mare. But he wasn't about to tell them that. He couldn't even imagine who could have pointed him out when he himself didn't even know he was going to do this. How could he tell anyone this, though? He would look crazy.

Sergeant Smith looked at his phone and showed agent Nunez. They both looked at Gabriel. Sergeant Smith slid the phone over in front of Gabriel. There was a photo on the phone.

"Gabriel, do you know what that is a picture of?"

The tears welled up in Gabriel's eyes. He couldn't answer. Instead, he nod-ded his head.

"Can you please tell us what it is and why you did it?"

Gabriel could hardly breathe. He didn't understand who would have done that. He knew he wouldn't have.

"It's my computer. I... I didn't do that. There is no way I would have done that! My dad and I built it together!"

Mrs. Ingles gasped and grabbed the phone.

"He would never do that! Someone must have broken into our house."

"Mrs. Ingles, please. You promised no outbursts."

Sergeant Smith continued the line of questioning.

"Gabriel, you smashed your cell phone, along with your computer. When was the last time you remember having your phone?"

"When I brought my sisters across the street. My Mom had texted me before we left the house to remind me to take my medication."

"What medication are you taking?"

"An antidepressant. The therapist I go to prescribed it about two months ago."

"What were you prescribed it for?"

"Depression. After my dad died and we moved, my mom didn't like that I had no friends, so she made me go see a shrink."

"Did it help?"

"I guess so. For the longest time, I felt nothing. I just felt numb. Until yester-day."

"What happened yesterday?"

"I skipped rocks at the pond before school and I missed my dad. I started to cry and feel sad. Then at school, some kids threw jello at the table I was sitting at. It got all over a girl's white t-shirt and it agitated me that people were such jerks."

"So that's why you wanted to shoot the school today? Because of the jerks."

"No. I already told you! I didn't want to hurt anyone!"

Gabriel's head was pounding. He was exhausted, and he still reeked of urine.

"I think we are done with this inter-view for now."

"Can I go home?"

"I am afraid not, kid. We will have to hold you overnight until your arraign-ment hearing. If the judge sets bail and your mom can post it, then you will go home. More than likely, you'll be under house arrest. But since you aren't cooperating, I am not sure the judge will set bail."

"But I am cooperating! I have told you the truth about everything!"

Gabriel's mom could hug him before they led him out of the room. He would spend the night in the holding cell. They took off the handcuffs when they put him in the cell and gave him a set of prison garb to change into. Once he was in clean clothes, he lay on the cot in the cell and cried himself to sleep.

CHAPTER ELEVEN

DERIC FELL ASLEEP, NOT worried about having a nightmare for the first time in his life. As he drifted into the dream state, he found himself inside what appeared to be a prison cell. As he turned around, he realized he was not alone. There on a cot in the cell was the sandy-haired boy from his school shooting dream. Deric stiffened, not knowing why he was having another dream about this kid.

The kid sat on the cot, staring at Deric. He looked frightened, and his eyes were bloodshot and puffy. It appeared as if he had been crying. This was a stark contrast to how he had looked in the other dream. Deric was confused, and it startled him when the boy spoke to him.

"Hey, you are the kid from my nightmare. You yelled at me to stop."

"Wait, you had a nightmare too? But aren't you the one that was doing the shooting?"

"In the nightmares, yes, I was the shooter. I was terrified of the dreams I was having. I thought they were just dreams."

"So you didn't want to kill everyone in your school?"

"No way, I have no reason to. I suppose you were the one that tipped the cops off about me?"

Deric didn't know whether he could trust this kid. It was also hard to know whether this was an actual conversation. He knew it was a dream, but this seemed so real. He tried to change the subject.

"How are we doing this? I mean, I know I am dreaming. I assume you are too. Are we communicating in our sleep?"

"I don't know. This is all so surreal. All I know is I was having the same recurring nightmare for weeks, then the other night it changed. You were in it, and you yelled at me to stop shooting. You saved me from shooting Adeline. When I awoke, I was happy you stopped me. But then the next day, they arrested me with a loaded gun and I don't remember how or where I got it."

"Adeline, the girl with the braids?"

"Yes, she has always been so nice to me. She is the closest thing to a friend

I have at school. So you remember the nightmare, too?"

"I remember, and yes, I told the police. I am glad I did too. You would have killed everyone in that building."

"Thank you. I didn't want to hurt anyone. Honest. I don't even remember anything. How I got the gun or even the walk to school? The police showed me pictures of my computer at home. I smashed it to pieces. They think I did that. I would never have destroyed it. My dad and I built it together before he died. I can't believe it's gone."

"Wow, dude. I am sorry about your computer. So what do you remember?"

"I remember bringing my little sisters across the street to the neighbor's house like I do every single morning before school. And then next thing I know, I am on the ground in pain. They had tased me, apparently."

"Ouch, so you don't remember smashing your computer or bringing a loaded gun to school?"

"No. The police think I am lying, and I am not cooperating, but I am telling the truth. I didn't tell them I was having a recurring nightmare about shooting up the school, though. I think that would make me look more guilty or crazy. Or maybe even both."

"I understand that feeling. I was afraid the police wouldn't believe me about you because I didn't know your name. There was some uncertainty even about what school you were from. It took some detective work. Thankfully, I guessed correctly. But I couldn't very well tell the police I dreamt about you."

"Yeah, I guess you couldn't. They asked me about who my accomplice was. Who ratted me out? I didn't even know for sure it was you, but you were the only difference in my last dream. So I figured it was you."

"Did you tell them?"

"No way! They would think I was crazy."

"I still don't understand how we are doing this. It is all crazy. But I believe you when you say you didn't want to hurt anyone and you don't remember. I wish I could help you more."

"I don't understand either. But I am glad that we have talked. It's good to know I have someone on my side."

"I hope we can figure it all out and get you set free. By the way, my name is Deric. What is yours?"

"Mine is Gabriel Ingles. You can call me Gabe."

"It was good chatting, Gabe. Good Luck."

Deric's alarm went off. As he awoke, he remembered his dream. He wrote everything down, recalling his conversation with the boy who called himself Gabe. The conversation was so realistic. The press hadn't released the name of the potential shooter, so where would his sub-conscience mind come up with that name? He would have to wait and see if they revealed the kid's name to see if the dream was real or just a figment of his imagination.

It was Friday, and he was just happy that it was the end of the school week. At school, everyone was still abuzz about the capture of the potential school shooter in California. Even though it was 3,000 miles away. This happened every time there was a school shooting or even a threat of a school shooting. Ever since Columbine.

Everyone had their theories. It had to be because of bullying, which was the biggest one. Then there were people talking that it was because of easy access to guns. Some people blamed violent video games and movies. Then Deric overheard a conversation between two teachers.

"You know, we didn't have this issue as much when we went to school. What has changed?"

"True, we had rifle clubs in our schools growing up, yet no one shot up the schools."

"The amount of people, especially adolescents being treated for depression and anxiety with antidepressants has risen though. I wonder if there is a connection?"

"That's an interesting thought. I never even considered that."

Deric remembered the look in Gabe's eyes in the nightmare compared to the look in his eyes in the dream he had last night. There was definitely a difference, but he couldn't quite pinpoint it. Could he have been on drugs? He said his dad had died. Maybe he was being treated for depression. If he had another dream with Gabe in it, maybe he could ask him. That's if the dream was even real.

When Deric got home from school, he turned the TV on. He normally wouldn't watch the television, however, he was craving any news to confirm that the conversation he had in his dream was real or fake. As he sat channel surfing, a breaking news update flashed across the screen. It was a press conference regarding the attempted school shooting.

The arraignment of the suspect occurred. They charged him as an adult. Since the student was being treated as a grownup and not a minor, they could release his name. When the news outlet said the suspect's name was Gabriel Ingles, Deric froze. The dream was real. The conversation he had with Gabe was authentic.

He watched the footage of Gabe being escorted from the courthouse into a corrections van. The kid looked terrified. Deric felt his stomach tighten as guilt crept through his body. He put Gabe behind bars. If he didn't, though, many innocent people would have died.

CHAPTER TWELVE

M RS. INGLES DROVE HOME in a daze. When she pulled into the drive-way, a detective met her when she exited her car.

"We are all done searching your home, ma'am. Here are your keys. Thank you for cooperating with us."

"No problem."

She didn't know what else to say. There were neighbors standing on the sidewalks watching. Mrs. Steven walked over with the girls. They

hugged their mother and started crying. Maria started the questions first.

"Why are the cops in our house?"

Then Kaira joined in.

"Where is Gabe, mom?"

Mrs. Ingles ushered the girls into the house while motioning for Mrs. Steven to come inside as well.

"Let's go inside and talk."

When they were inside and seated in the living room, Mrs. Ingles explained where Gabriel was and what had hap-pened. Both of Gabriel's sisters were sobbing. Mrs. Steven tried to help their mother console them. They final-ly calmed down enough to have some dinner that Mrs. Steven had whipped up for the family.

As they were sitting at the table, Mrs. Ingles broke the silence.

"Girls, I have to ask you some questions, and I need your honest answers."

Maria and Kaira stared at their mother wide-eyed with their mouths full of food. As they swallowed, they looked at each other and shrugged their shoulders. Kaira was feeling guilty about not being honest with Gabriel or their mom the day before, so she was eager to show her mom cooperation.

"Sure mom."

"Did Gabe seem off this morning?"

Maria was also feeling guilty about giving Gabriel a hard time in the morning.

"No, mom. He was a little grumpy at me because I didn't want to go to school today, but nothing unusual."

"Why didn't you want to go to school today?"

Maria looked at Kaira, who nodded her head to her sister.

"This girl Betsy said she was gonna beat me up because I like this boy Mike and so does she."

Mrs. Ingles put her hand to her forehead.

"Why didn't you tell me?"

"I didn't want to worry you, mom, or Gabe."

"So Gabe didn't know you were having trouble with a bully?"

"No."

"Okay, I will call the school tomorrow about that issue. Is there anything else you can think of about Gabe and this morning?"

Kaira looked at her and bit her lip.

"Well, as he was going down Mrs. Steven's steps, he stopped. He pulled out his phone, put it back in his pocket, and instead of heading to school, he went back home. I just figured you texted him to take his meds."

"Okay, I did text him. Is there anything else?"

Mrs. Ingles knew it wasn't her text though because Gabriel had said that he remembered receiving her reminder text before dropping his sisters off at the neighbor's house. She would mention this to Sergeant Smith.

"I watched for him to come back out of the house. When he did, he had an angry look on his face. I have never seen him like that before. Then he walked down to the park entrance and went in there. But that isn't unusual. He always goes to the park before and after school if he has time."

Kaira paused and then continued.

"I watched for him to come out of the park. When he did, he had a different backpack. His backpack is blue and the one he had was black."

It surprised Mrs. Ingles. Gabriel went into the park with his blue backpack and came out with a black one. She knew the police had found him with the black backpack. It had extra ammunition in it and an extra gun beside the one he had in his hand when they tased him.

"Are you sure it was a different backpack?"

"Yes, mom. I am sure. It seemed odd to me that's why I remember."

"Thank you for telling me. I am going to call Sergeant Smith and let him know. Maybe someone saw him in the park. Maybe someone saw him pick up the wrong backpack. This could all be a misunderstanding."

Mrs. Ingles left the room to call the police station. Sergeant Smith appreciated her phone call and the information. He was sending detectives to the park to search for Gabriel's blue backpack and any other evidence. He would be in contact with her and would take an official statement from Kaira in the morning.

It was time for the girls to go to bed, and Mrs. Steven stayed until they were asleep. She gave Mrs. Ingles a hug before she left.

"Everything is going to be okay. Gabe is a good boy."

"Thank you. The girls won't be going to school tomorrow, but if I need you to watch them while I go to Gabe's court appearance, can you?"

"Yes, absolutely."

"Thank you."

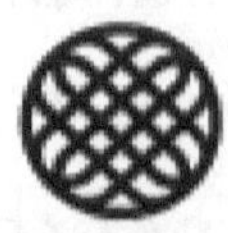

CHAPTER THIRTEEN

G ABRIEL AWOKE TO THE coldness of the holding cell he had been sleeping in. The cot was lumpy and hard. He missed the warm comfort of his bed. The dream he had perplexed him. He had a conversation with Deric, the boy, that had appeared in his last nightmare.

The same boy who stopped him from killing Adeline. He found out he had stopped him from killing anyone. For that, he was forever grateful. However, he was still in jail and most likely facing a lifetime in prison. For something he doesn't even remember doing.

It bothered him that there was a gap in his memory. He had never had that happen before. As he contemplated everything that had happened in the last 48 hours, he bit at his fingernails. His leg bounced, and he stopped when an officer came to get him.

"Your lawyer is here to meet with you before your arraignment hearing."

They brought Gabriel to the interrogation room, where Mr. Whitty was already sitting at the table.

"Good morning Gabriel. There have been some developments in your case."

"Good morning, Sir. Developments? Good or bad?"

"Yes, a witness has come forward. Your sister Maria. Apparently, you received a text message after dropping your sisters off while you were on the steps. Do you remember who texted you and what it was about?"

"No sir, the only text I remember getting was the one from my mom reminding me to take my pill."

"She then saw you go back into your house. When you came out, you seemed angry. Then she saw you go into the park down the street. You went in with your blue backpack and came out with the black backpack."

"Okay. I don't remember any of that. I go to the park and skip rocks almost every day before school. Maybe I picked up someone else's backpack instead of my own?"

"The police found your blue backpack with your books and personal items in the park. In some bushes. Hidden. That suggests premeditation in their eyes and in the district attorneys. That along with your destroyed computer and cell phone. Things do not look good. They are going to charge you as an adult. I think our best bet is to work a temporary insanity plea deal."

Gabriel lifted his handcuffed hands to his face. His eyes burned with the threat of tears waiting to spill over.

"What happens if I plead temporary insanity?"

"We might avoid a lifetime prison sentence. I would try to get you placed into a mental health facility for treatment instead. You don't have a record, so that is in your favor. A court-appointed psychiatrist will evaluate you. I have to tell you, they want to use you to set an example. So they are going to come at you hard regardless of your clean record."

"So you are basically telling me I am facing life in prison or life in a mental health facility?"

"No, I would try to get you a ten-year sentence in the mental health facility. I think the plea deal is the best for all involved, kid. But, it's your choice. You can plead not guilty and go to trial or you can plead guilty with temporary insanity."

"Honestly, I feel insane. I don't understand what is happening. I can't remember a chunk of time in my life. And my family doesn't need the drama of a trial. I will try the plea deal."

The arraignment went as planned. Gabriel's lawyer pleaded guilty by reason of insanity. The court transferred the case from juvenile court to adult court. He was being charged as an adult. Gabriel would get transferred to a high-security mental health facility for evaluation and incarceration. Pending the evaluation, they would consider the plea deal. If the evaluation showed he was competent, he would stand trial.

They led Gabriel out of the courthouse, where there were throngs of reporters and media outlets covering his story. He tried covering his face with his handcuffed hands. Bystanders yelled obscenities at him and called him an evil monster. All he could think about was the look on his mother's face. This broke her more than she had been when his father died. Gabriel was worried about his mom and his sisters.

When the van stopped, Gabriel's heart thumped hard in his chest. It had been a long ride. His lawyer had advised him he would meet with the court-appointed psychiatrist after arriving at the facility. The corrections officer guided him into a brick building with sterile-looking walls and hallways. The brightness of it all hurt his eyes. An orderly took over after going through a secured door.

They brought Gabriel into a private room, where they patted him down before having the handcuffs removed. The orderly gave him a set of hospital-style scrubs to wear and advised Gabriel to change his clothes. When the orderly left the room, locking the door behind him, Gabriel just stood there. The realization that this was his reality hit him hard. He felt dizzy and grabbed onto a counter to steady himself. He composed himself and changed clothes. The scrubs were semi-comfortable, yet slightly baggy on his slim frame.

The orderly returned and guided Gabriel to another room. This one had a leather couch and an enormous desk. There was a short, stout man with circular glasses sitting on the tip of his nose sitting behind it. His white coat made Gabriel deduce he was the psychiatrist he would talk with.

"Good afternoon, Gabriel. My name is Doctor Slocum. I will evaluate you for the court. Rest assured, I will know if you are trying to fool everyone with this temporary insanity."

"Good afternoon. Sir, I am not trying to fool anyone. I can't remember a chunk of time in my life. The moments leading up to my being arrested. So yes, I feel insane."

Doctor Slocum leaned forward on his desk, intently gazing at Gabriel.

"You say you don't remember what happened that day?"

"No, sir. I remember dropping my little sisters off at the neighbor's house and then the next thing I recall is being on the ground after being tased."

"Interesting. Would you be agreeable to a lie detector test?"

"Yes, I want to prove that I didn't do this."

"But Gabriel, they arrested you with a loaded gun in your hand and a backpack loaded with another gun and ammunition. You did this."

"Sir, how can I do something and not remember it? I can remember bits of my life when I was a young child, but I can't remember how I got the guns and ammunition and what I was going to do with them. It makes little sense to me."

"Well, son, the trauma of being tased and arrested might have given you a form of amnesia. I can try hypnosis to unlock your subconscious memories. I have to warn you though if I unlock the memories of how you got the weapons and your intentions, I am required to inform the court."

"Doc, do what you need to do. I want to know the truth. If you can unlock it, I will gladly suffer the consequences."

"Gabriel, I have to say, you are one of the most agreeable patients I have encountered here. That counts for something with me."

The doctor asked Gabriel a bunch of questions and then had the orderly take Gabriel to his room. In the morning, Doctor Slocum would perform the lie detector test and then he would try hypnosis. Gabriel lay on his bed and cried himself to sleep.

PART TWO

"**M**IRACLES START TO HAPPEN when you give as much energy to your dreams as you do to your fears."
~ Richard Wilkins

CHAPTER FOURTEEN

IN AN OFFICE IN Long Beach, a man in a black suit sat at an enormous mahogany desk drumming his fingers. He was listening to the other person on the other end of the telephone.

"Sir, they apprehended the subject. The boy could not carry out the act. He claims he did not know what he was doing and remembers nothing."

The man, listening, paused the drumming of his fingers, contemplating what he was just told.

"You say the kid remembers not a thing?"

"Yes, sir. His attorney has entered a plea deal with the district attorney claiming temporary insanity. They have moved him to a mental health institution to undergo psychiatric evaluation. What do you want me to do?"

"I want you to monitor the situation. As long as he remembers bupkis, the program is not at risk and we can go about our business as usual. Do not contact me unless the kid remembers. You understand?"

"Yes, sir."

Hanging up the phone, the man entwined his hands and folded them in his lap as he swiveled his chair to look out the window. He sat there contemplating the information he had received. The news had shown the arrest and arraignment of the boy. One piece of information bothered him. If the boy had no memory of the incident, how were the police able to intercept his plan? On the news, they stated there was an anonymous tip. If the kid had told someone, that was a liability.

They needed to know who tipped off the authorities. He should have told his informant to work on that. Tracking down who was to blame for the plan being foiled. He knew his job was on the line if he didn't produce results. Those who hired him demanded certain outcomes. When they didn't occur, they made threats. Promises he knew they would keep. The phone calls had already started coming in with the hard questions. It was a delicate balance of keeping his clients happy without bringing suspicion upon himself or his program from the outside.

His clients wanted better results. They even wanted him to step up his program and make the incidents occur more frequently. He tried but was ineffective at explaining more frequent occurrences would draw too much suspicion. With this failed mission, though, they were demanding another undertaking soon.

The others weren't ready yet. Something had gone wrong with this operative and he couldn't chance having the same thing happen. He needed more information on what went wrong. He picked up the phone and dialed.

The voice on the other end answered.

"Hey boss, I thought you didn't want contact right now?"

"Look, I have been thinking. Who was the informant?"

"The authorities do not know."

"Find out. That is a loose end that needs to be tied up before the program can proceed. We do not know what that informant knows."

"I will do my best, sir."

CHAPTER FIFTEEN

DERIC HADN'T HAD A nightmare or dream in weeks. He worried about Gabriel. There had been no news about his case after the arraignment. Typical of the news cycle, the next big story was some celebrity causing a stir and being canceled. The only good thing that had happened was now he slept well. He was no longer afraid of sleeping. The anxiety he had felt about it had resolved. His grades were even improving, since his brain wasn't in the constant fog of sleeplessness and angst.

His morning went as was typical until he walked into homeroom. There was a new student. A girl. The same girl he saved in the dream with Gabriel. Pinching the top of his hand and flinching when he felt the pain. He realized he was not dreaming. What was she doing here, in his school? Gabriel had told him her name was Adeline.

When the homeroom teacher introduced her to the class as Adeline Degroot, Deric knew she was indeed the same girl. Why was she here? Adeline smiled as she sat down at a desk right across the aisle from Deric. Was there a look of acknowledgment on her face? Was she aware of him in the dream as well?

It wasn't until lunch that he could actually talk to her. He purposely sat with her. Marco sat with him too, so he would have to ask generic questions.

"Hi, my name is Deric. How is your first day going?"

"Hi, my name is Adeline. It is going fine. Thank you for asking."

"Can I ask you where you moved from?"

"Of course. We moved from Long Beach, California. My dad is in the Navy. He is an instructor, and they transferred him to the New London Sub Base. So we had to move."

"Wow, that is a long way to move from. Isn't Long Beach where that school shooting almost happened and they arrested that kid?"

"Yeah, that was my old school. It was a scary, weird thing. Gabe wasn't the type of kid you would think would want to do something like that. He was quiet, but he was nice."

Deric confirmed his suspicions. She was the same girl, and she knew Gabriel. By the way she looked at Marco cautiously, she knew why he was asking. He had to think of a way to talk to her alone.

"I bet it was scary. I can't even imagine. Hey, if you want to talk or hang out, I can give you my cell phone number."

Marco looked back and forth at the exchange between Deric and Adeline. He couldn't believe his ears. Deric was giving out his cell phone number to a girl. It was already out of character for Deric to be talking to someone outside his tiny friend's circle, let alone a girl. A beautiful girl at that. Marco elbowed their friend Travis.

"Our little boy is growing up."

Travis and Marcos busted into laughter as Deric's cheeks flushed with embarrassment. Adeline blushed as well.

"I would love to hang out, so sure you can give me your cell number."

Travis and Marco stopped laughing. They sat in amazement. As the lunch bell rang signaling their time was up, they all cleaned their table and headed back to class. Deric was pleased to find that Adeline was in the rest of his classes. When it was time to get on the bus to go home, he was even more surprised to find her on his bus.

He slid into the seat across from her.

"Hey, you live in Preston too?"

"Yes, my parents rented a house on Parks Road. They wanted the country setting."

"Wow, what a coincidence. I live on that road! We are neighbors."

Adeline smiled and engaged Deric in small talk about the town of Preston. It wasn't until they got off the bus and started walking down the road to their houses that she broached the subject they both had been wanting to discuss.

"So, now that we are alone and there is no one else to hear our conversation, let's address the elephant in the room, shall we?"

Deric stopped in his tracks. This was it. This was what he had waited for all day to confirm.

"Sure, let's discuss what we both know. We have seen each other before."

"Yes, I had a nightmare the day before the attempted shooting at my old school. You were in the dream and saved my life! But how? And then Gabe actually attempted the school shooting, but the police caught him before he could hurt anyone. No one knows who it was that tipped the police off. It was you, wasn't it?"

"How did we all have the same dream? Yes, it was me that tipped off the police. You can't tell anyone, though. Obviously, we can't very well tell anyone I dreamt about the shooting before it happened and then tracked down the school. They would think I was crazy. Which I very well may be."

"Who else had the dream besides you and me? You said we all had the same dream."

"Gabe. Except he had been having the dream reoccurring for a month. It was always the same until I was in it and saved you. He didn't want to hurt anyone and didn't know why he was having the dream."

"Wait, how do you know all that about Gabe?"

Deric ran his fingers through his hair.

"I had another dream with him in jail the night before his arraignment. He doesn't remember even how he got the guns."

Adeline stood there, just staring at Deric. None of what they were discussing made sense. How could they all be in the same dreams? And talk to one another in their dreams?

Deric could see the confusion on Adeline's face. It sounded even crazier vocalizing all of it to someone else. Even though they didn't understand what was going on, they knew it was reality. They both experienced the dream. Finally, Adeline could say something else.

"I don't understand any of this. But I know it is all real because we experienced it. I agree though we can't tell anyone about it. And I promise not to tell anyone you are the informant."

"Yeah, I don't understand it all either. I mean, I have always had dreams that came true, but this was the first time I took action to stop them from happening. This is all new to me, being able to communicate in my dreams with others. I am worried about Gabe, though. There have not been anymore dreams with him since the night before his arraignment. I hope he is okay. Thanks for promising to keep my secret. It means a lot."

"Gabe was a nice kid. It never made sense to me, and now even more it is perplexing. I hope he is okay too. There has been little on the news about him. I will text some of my old friends and see if they have heard anything."

"That sounds like a great idea! Hopefully, you can get some information. Can I finish walking you home?"

"Absolutely!"

Deric and Adeline walked the rest of the way to her house, which was two houses down from his. Then he backtracked to his own house.

CHAPTER SIXTEEN

GABRIEL SAT IN THE courtroom next to his attorney. They were there for a pre-trial hearing. Today, they would provide evidence that support-ed their claim of temporary insanity in Gabriel's defense. In doing so, they hoped the court would agree to the plea deal and they would sentence Gabriel to ten years in the mental fa-cility.

His mother sat behind him, with her hands clasped together in silent prayer that her son would get the plea bargain. She had met with the lawyer the day before, who seemed hopeful that they had enough evidence to back their claim of temporary insanity.

People packed the courtroom, all interested in hearing the outcome of the case. Many hoped that Gabriel would not get the plea bargain. They felt he was competent and the court should try him as an adult to get the maximum penalty. They felt what he had done was equivalent to domestic terrorism.

Seargent Smith and Special Agent Nunez sat in the back of the courtroom. This case intrigued them both. The nagging question of who the accomplice was that tipped them off was another reason they were there. They hoped that something would lead them to the tipster's identity.

As they brought the court into session and the proceedings started, Gabriel fidgeted in his seat slightly. He felt uncomfortable with all eyes on him. It felt as though he was being pierced by a million little daggers when he peered around the room. To calm himself, he focused on the flag by the side of the judge.

The district attorney opened the case with the charges brought against Gabriel and stated there was proof of premeditation. Then Gabriel's attorney made his opening statement and how they would prove temporary insanity.

It was well into the proceedings when Doctor Slocum took the stand for questioning. Gabriel's attorney asked him the most important question first.

"In your professional opinion, do you believe Gabriel Ingles knew what he was doing on the day they accuse him of bringing a gun to school, intending to shoot everyone there?"

"After several sessions with Gabriel, mostly done through hypnosis, I can say without a doubt, he suffers from psychogenic amnesia, more specifically psychogenic fugue. The cause of amnesia is unknown. However, I have ruled out all neurological causes. He has no recollection of the events leading up to his arrest."

"So you state that, in fact, Gabriel has no memory of obtaining the weapons he was in possession of at the time of the arrest?"

"Yes, in fact, he has no memory of that day after dropping his sisters off at the neighbor's house."

"Does he have any memory of planning the shooting?"

"No. He has no memory of planning the shooting. However, he was having a reoccurring nightmare about doing the shooting for at least a month up to the day of the incident."

Gabriel's attorney rocked back on his heels and took his right hand out of his pocket. His next line of questioning would be important.

"So let me get this straight. You say Gabriel has no memory other than remembering a recurring dream he was having about shooting up his school? Wouldn't the dreams prove that this was pre-meditated?"

"Not necessarily. I questioned him under hypnosis and with a lie detector about the dreams. When I asked how he felt when he woke up from the dreams. He always stated he wasn't worried about them because he knew he didn't have access to any weapons and he had no reason to want to shoot up his school. Therefore, he never mentioned the dreams to anyone else."

"So in your professional opinion, you believe him when he says he had no intentions of shooting up his school, even though he was dreaming about doing just that."

"Yes, in my professional opinion, I believe him. I have had multiple sessions with him, and his story never falters. Gabriel has been under a great deal of emotional stress in the last year. He lost his father to a heart attack, moved from his childhood home, started a new school, and took on the role of the man of the house, helping his mother raise his two younger sisters. That is a lot for a sixteen-year-old to handle. His mother had brought him to a therapist, and he was taking medications to help with his depression. They were doing everything to manage the situation and the emotional stress healthily. I commend them for that. They were diligent in the medications he was taking as well. However, I also believe he suffered psychosis, which led to the incident they arrested him for, which in turn caused his psychogenic amnesia."

"One last question, doctor. Do you believe on the day of the alleged incident that Gabriel Ingles was in a normal state of cognition?"

"Absolutely not. I believe he was in the middle of a psychotic break."

"So you believe in your professional opinion Gabriel was suffering from temporary insanity?"

"Yes."

"I know I said the last question was my final one, but I have one more. Do you think you can treat Gabriel and return him to society to be a productive member of it?"

"Absolutely. I have never treated a patient so willing to do whatever it takes to heal their mind. "

"Your Honor, considering the doctor's testimony, the defense rests its case. We ask that you grant the plea bargain and sentence Gabriel to only ten years in a high-security psychiatric facility."

Gabriel watched as his attorney sat back down beside him. He was glad that his attorney hadn't pressed the doctor more about his dreams. The prosecuting attorney was getting up to question the doctor. This made his stomach flip. He knew the dreams made him look guilty. It was in hindsight he wished he had told someone, anyone, about them. Maybe then it would be easier to prove he really had no reason or desire to shoot up his school.

The prosecutor stood in front of the witness stand.

"Sir, you have stated that it is your professional opinion that Gabriel Ingles suffered a psychotic break because of the emotional stress and trauma he endured in the last year, correct?"

"Yes."

"You also stated that Gabriel admits he had been having recurring dreams of shooting up his school, correct?"

"Yes."

"But you say Gabriel told no one of these dreams. Am I recalling your words correctly?"

"Yes."

"Then how could an anonymous caller inform both the Long Beach police department and the FBI of Gabriel's plan?"

Gabriel squirmed in his seat. This was the line of questioning he feared. Not for himself, but for Deric.

"Well, sir, when asked about that under hypnosis, Gabriel's answer was the day before the incident, the reoccurring dream changed. Another boy stopped him from shooting a girl he really liked, which he was happy about. He thought his medications were working, and that was why his dream was changing. Gabriel also told me he had another dream with the same boy after his arrest. The boy claimed to be the one who called the authorities."

"Am I hearing you correctly? You are saying a boy from Gabriel's dreams is the anonymous tipster? Do you honestly believe that?"

"Yes, that is what Gabriel told me. Again, his story never changed, whether under hypnosis or with the lie detector. He was telling the truth. However, I have an explanation. I believe Gabriel's psychosis also caused him to suffer from a disassociative identity disorder. In other words, he was also the other boy in the dreams. Which means he was the one who called in the tips to the authorities."

"Sir, are you saying Gabriel called the authorities on himself?"

"Yes, I believe he did."

"Did he give a name to this other identity?"

"Yes. He named the other boy Deric."

"And you are sure he has no friends with that name?"

"I am positive. I even researched the names of all the kids in both his old school and new school. There was not a single kid in either school with the name Deric. The fact that this identity showed up in his dreams also lends credence to my theory. How else could someone from his dreams inform the authorities about what in his dream he was going to do? Gabriel admitted the dreams were not his true thoughts. Telling on himself makes sense if he subconsciously feared it would somehow come true."

"Thank you, Doctor Slocum. Your Honor, considering the doctor's testimony and the fact Gabriel has no priors, the state will agree to the plea bargain of temporary insanity. We recommend the defendant to be remanded to The Priformal Institute under Doctor Slocum's care for the duration of the next ten years."

Gabriel let out a sigh of relief. Although he could hear his mother sobbing softly behind him. The mental institute was much better than the prison. Before they led him out of the courtroom, he received a hug from his mom. When her arms wrapped around him, his eyes welled up with tears.

"I will be okay, mom. I love you."

"I love you too, Gabe."

Sergeant Smith and Special Agent Nunez exited the courtroom. This was a first for them both. The perpetrator had supposedly called on himself. While it seemed crazy and farfetched, it seemed more plausible than the alternative. That some kid in Gabriel's dream had called on him. To believe that, one would have to believe in psychic powers or some other supernatural happenings. They were both men of facts, cold hard tangible facts.

CHAPTER SEVENTEEN

THE MAN SAT IN his office with his back to the door, staring out his window over the city. His clients were getting restless, they wanted results. The program was still on pause due to not knowing who had contacted the authorities. When the phone rang, he swung his chair around to answer it.

"Hello, this is Mitch speaking. May I ask who is calling?"

"Hey boss, it's me."

"I hope you are calling for a good reason."

Mitch drummed his fingers on his desk.

"Yes, sir. I just got back from the courthouse. I was observing the pre-trial of that kid."

"AND?"

"Well, it seems as if he called the authorities on himself. A psychiatrist claimed something about a unique identity during his testimony. During his sessions with the doctor, the kid had spoken about having a recurring dream, but then the day before it was different, and this other kid stopped him. Apparently, he claims the same kid was in a dream he had after being arrested and admitted to him he called the police. The psychiatrist claimed the kid was crazy. The court agreed to the temporary insanity deal and sent him back to the institute for the next ten years."

"Interesting. Did the kid have a name for this other identity?"

"Yeah, I think it was Deric."

"So the court believes he is crazy, and this was some sort of alter ego?"

"Yes."

"Good work."

"Thanks, Boss. Do you want to resume the program?"

"Yes. Start working with the other subjects. We are behind schedule."

Mitch hung up the phone. It was a relief they could resume the program. It would get his clients off his back. He would have to do a better job at screening who they put in the program, though. This kid had no indications of having any kind of identity disorder. They would have to make sure none of the other participants showed signs of having this type of disorder. He couldn't risk them telling the authorities about themselves, too.

CHAPTER EIGHTEEN

ADELINE HAD GONE OVER to Deric's house to work on a homework assignment she was having trouble with. They were sitting in the living room with the TV on. A breaking news announcement came across the screen. Both Deric and Adeline jumped when they mentioned Gabriel's name. It was an update on what had occurred at his pre-trial and how they had found him temporarily insane.

They both felt a mixture of sadness and relief. At least Gabriel wasn't going to jail. However, spending ten years in a mental institute didn't sound fun, either. They said nothing about the informant. Deric was relieved about that.

"I guess they have forgotten all about the tipster."

"Luckily for you, right?"

"Yeah. I feel bad for Gabe, though."

"Are you sorry you told the authorities?"

"No way! Even Gabe was glad I did. So many people would have died, including you."

Deric grabbed her hand and continued.

"I couldn't have lived with that."

Adeline blushed.

"Well, I am happy to be alive and to have met you in person."

"I am happy I saved your life in my dream and in real life!"

They finished their homework, and Deric walked her back home. When he went to bed, he fell asleep rather quickly.

He awoke, and straight away realized he was in a dream. Looking around, he noticed he was in a movie theatre. Not one he had ever been in before, so he started to figure out where he was. He looked up at the movie screen. It was playing the previews. Every seat was full in the theatre, indicating a sold-out show. Standing up, he moved from his seat. No one seemed to notice. They were all just part of the dream.

Then he noticed someone moving from a seat a few rows down from him. He squinted to see better. His heart raced. What was Adeline doing in his dream? She was looking straight at him and walking towards him.

"Where are we, Deric?"

"I don't know. We are in a dream, though I know that for sure and it will not be a good one. They never are."

"This is weird. Like none of these people can see us or talk to us, they don't seem to notice we are even here."

"Yeah, this is how most of my dreams have been, except for the one with you and Gabe."

The door interrupted their conversation. It slammed open. As they both looked up, the loud thunder of gunshots rang out, and flashes of light illuminated the darkness with each round shot. Screams rang out. Deric and Adeline ran toward the shooter, knowing they couldn't die. They both yelled at the same time.

"Stop!!!"

The boy with the gun stopped and looked at them both. He heard them. Deric got an idea.

"Why are you doing this?"

"They told me to."

"Who are they?"

"The voices in my head."

"What is your name?"

"Matthew."

"What is your last name?"

"Matthew Nicholson, what's it to you?"

"I want to help you."

"Nobody can help me. This is my mission."

"Okay, where are you from?"

"Patterson, New Jersey."

"That's where we are now, right?"

"Yes stupid. We are at The Hoyt Cinemas. Now let me finish my job."

The boy raised his gun and continued to shoot everyone in the theatre except Deric and Adeline. They stood and watched the carnage unfold in front of them, not able to stop what was happening. Deric grabbed Adeline's hand.

"It's okay. We are going to stop this from happening."

"How?"

"I got enough information to call the authorities. As long as they believe me, they should be able to catch him and stop him before he hurts anyone."

"I hope so."

Adeline squeezed Deric's hand and then Deric awakened in his room. No shooter and no Adeline. It did not scare him like in the past with these types of dreams. It was too early in the morning to call the authorities. Just as he rolled over to fall back asleep, his cell phone dinged, notifying him of a text message. He grabbed his phone. It was from Adeline.

Are you awake?

Yes.

Did we just really dream that same dream?

Yup.

What the hell? That is so weird.

Welcome to my world.

What are you going to do?

Skip school and call the authorities from the pay phone down the road.

Can I join you?

Sure, I will text you when everyone leaves for work.

Sounds like a plan.

After everyone in his house had gone to work, Deric texted Adeline. She met him at the end of his driveway and they rode their bikes to the same pay phone Deric had used before. He called the local police, the state police, and the FBI office in New Jersey. They prayed it was enough to stop the actual shooting from taking place. Now all they could do was wait.

Deric and Adeline hung out at his house for the rest of the day. She went home before anyone from Deric's family or her family got home. As Deric sat in the living room with his mom and dad watching the news, his palms started to sweat and his stomach cramped up. What if the authorities didn't believe him this time?

A breaking news bulletin flashed across the screen of the television. Deric sat up straighter and listened carefully as the newscaster reported that an eighteen-year-old boy by the name of Matthew Nicholson was in custody in Patterson, New Jersey, where he allegedly was planning on committing a mass shooting at the Hoyt Cinemas. Authorities had received an anonymous tip about the plans and were successful in intercepting Mr. Nicholson before he hurt anyone.

Deric breathed a sigh of relief. He killed no one. And Deric was still unknown. His cell phone dinged with an incoming text notification and he grabbed it and headed to his bedroom.

Did you see the news?

Yeah. It worked again.

Thank God. I was worried all day!

Me too. I will see you at school tomorrow.

Yup. See you tomorrow.

Deric went to sleep and slept like a baby.

CHAPTER NINETEEN

MITCH WATCHED THE TELEVISION screen and swirled the whiskey in his glass round and round. The news coming across the screen wasn't good for his program. In a month's time, they had caught two candidates. The program's subjects usually avoided apprehension. They always completed their mission by committing suicide.

The apprehension of a second liege put the program in total jeopardy. He needed to pause it again. Who was the

tipster that kept notifying the authorities? There had to be an inside leak
or informant within the program. He
was foolish to believe that the first kid
had multiple identities and called on
himself.

With this new arrest, there needed to be a new plan. Mitch knew he
needed to gain access to both Gabriel
and Matthew. He couldn't leave them
to the authorities. They incarcerated
Gabriel in a mental institute in which
it would be easier to extricate him.
Matthew, on the other hand, was in
the beginning stages of the judicial
process. He would have more security
measures surrounding him.

Mitch picked up the phone and dialed
it.

"Hello?"

"It's me. I need you to put together
two extraction teams."

"Sure thing, boss. Who are the targets?"

"Who do you think? The program is in jeopardy if we leave those two out there. And as of this minute, the program is on pause again. We can not risk being exposed."

"Okay, boss. I will put together two teams. When I have them assembled, I will call you. Then you can set up a meeting and go over your directives with each one."

"Yes. Let me know when you have them assembled."

Mitch slammed the phone down. Pouring another glass of whiskey, he knew the calls would come in from his clients at any moment now. He needed to reassure them he had everything under control. But he wasn't exactly sure he did.

Just as he was going to pick up the phone to call another contact, it rang. Looking at the caller id, he swigged the rest of his whisky and answered.

"Hello, this is Mitch."

"Mitch, I am sure you recognize who this is and you know why I am calling."

"Yes, sir. I know. Look, I know you need certain results. We have given you those results before, so I trust you will understand we are doing everything in our power to mitigate the situation."

"There are billions of dollars at stake here, Mitch. If you can't produce results, we are going to have to go to someone else."

"Who are you going to go to? There is no one with the expertise that I have. Anyone else will be a crap shoot. If you think we have a situation now, just try going with some amateur. The results will be catastrophic."

"Trust me, Mitch, there are other experts that have been soliciting us. They know our agenda. They are more than willing to help for the right price."

"If you are talking about foreign actors, I have warned you in the past about them. Do what you want, though. My program is on hold until further notice. Unless, of course, you want us to all go down with the two suspects?"

"No, of course, we don't want exposure. But we need certain results. We have a limited timeframe here."

"You don't think I know that? Give me a couple of weeks. We are working on a plan now to tie up the already loose ends. If I can't get it done, then I will relinquish the program and end it completely."

"You have one month. One month to tidy up this mess. If it's not done in a month, your contract will end, and so will you."

"Are you threatening me?"

"No, Mitch, I am stating the facts. We don't leave loose ends that can come back to bite us. You should realize that. This is a high-stakes game. No holds barred. Have a good night. I hope you get the situation resolved. I really do."

The silence on the other end infuriated Mitch more than he already was. The bastard had threatened him and then hung up on him. He picked up the glass and hurled it into his fireplace. Glass shattered inside the hearth into tiny shards.

Those boys were the key. He sat at his computer and pulled up both their files to see if there was any connection. Could they have been in the same online gaming rooms? He logged into the gaming chat rooms he used to help bolster his connection with the subjects. Anything that might point him toward who they both told. After hours of research, Mitch found nothing linking the boys.

His thoughts went back to a leak in the program. He had been so careful with whom he employed and had vetted personally each member. The team knew he had dirt on them. It was his assurance of no double-crossing. There was no one he could even fathom jeopardizing what they were doing. He pored over the associates in his files. It was early in the morning when he had concluded it wasn't anyone within the program.

CHAPTER TWENTY

GABRIEL WAS IN THE common room, the television was on. Around the room, patients dispersed and engaged in various activities. A few orderlies watched carefully. He was sitting across from another patient with whom he was playing chess when the breaking news banner caught his attention on the tv screen.

They caught another potential mass shooter before he could carry out the assault. Again, they mentioned an anonymous tipster. This made Gabriel smile. Deric must have had another dream. He was happy his new friend could use his gift to save lives. It had been weeks since they shared their last dream. He wished he could talk to Deric again. Just to reassure him, he was okay.

Then it hit him. What if the authorities caught on that he didn't call on himself? Would that change his plea deal? More importantly, though, would that put Deric in harm's way? Gabriel knew he had told his doctor about the dreams and gave him Deric's name. Thankfully, he didn't know Deric's last name. He was sure that because of that fact, Deric would be safe. At least for a little while.

Seven o'clock came fast in the institute and they rounded Gabriel up, along with the other patients, for their meds and bedtime. When the click of the door latching behind him signaled they locked him in, Gabriel spit out his meds into his hand and stuffed them under his mattress. The day they arrested him, he had stopped taking his meds. In doing so, his mind seemed clearer than it had been in the month leading up to his incarceration.

He hoped that eventually, his memory would return. In his dreams, he was having flashes of memory, but every time he thought they were coming back, he would wake up. The most frequent and painful memory he was getting flashes of was him taking a hammer to his computer. This still baffled him. That computer was his pride and joy. The last thing he and his dad had done together was build it. It made little sense to him that he would smash it to pieces.

As he drifted off to sleep, he remembered the day he built it alongside his dad. They joked and laughed while completing each task. It was one of his cherished memories.

It was the click of his door being unlocked that awakened him. The darkness filled his room and the only light came from his door opening into the hallway. He could tell it was earlier than normal. The overnight orderly was the one unlocking the door. There alongside him stood three men. Two in black suits and one in a white lab coat. Gabriel rubbed his eyes to help them adjust.

"Gabriel, you are being transferred into my care. Doctor Reingold is my name. I am taking you to my facility. I gave the paperwork to the orderly here. Everything has gone through the courts. My colleagues will put you in handcuffs to be transported."

"Where is your facility? Does my mom know? Will she be able to visit?"

"It isn't far. Yes, your mother will visit and we have apprised her of the situation."

One man in a black suit approached Gabriel and handcuffed him. Then he escorted him out of his room and down the hallway. When they reached outside, it was still very dark. The men guided Gabriel into the back of a black van and seat-belted him to a bench in the back. They partitioned where he was sitting off from where the rest of the passengers were.

The ride to the new facility took a lot longer than Gabriel expected, although he slept on and off for most of the ride. He did not know the actual time they were on the road. His head was sore from the back of it, bumping against the wall of the van. The vehicle finally stopped and the back doors opened.

They seemed to be inside a giant cavern. Gabriel's heart raced. This wasn't a normal mental facility. Beads of sweat formed along his forehead and his palms felt moist. The two men unbuckled him and forcibly exited him from the van.

Another man met them. This one was wearing a grey pinstriped suit. He recognized him and didn't understand what he was doing in this place.

"Ah Gabriel, I am glad you are here, my boy. You will now be under my care again."

"What about Doctor Reingold? I thought he was taking over my care?"

"Yes, I see. There was a misunderstanding with my associate."

"Where am I?"

"You are in a top-secret institution. It is to help treat people like you with dissociative identity disorder and psychogenic amnesia. We are here to help you."

"What about my mom? And my sisters? Will they be able to visit?"

"In time, my boy. When we feel you are getting well enough."

Gabriel felt the tightness in his chest. His breathing quickened. None of this felt right. He felt like they had kidnapped him right under everyone's noses. The men in black suits grabbed him by the arms and pushed him towards a narrow passageway. Soon they came to a door that they punched a code into.

There was a hallway that looked very much like a hospital wing in front of them. They pushed Gabriel along until they came to another door. They opened it. It led to a small room with a cot, a toilet, and a sink. Gabriel got the impression this was his new home. The men took off the handcuffs and left him in the room, locking the door behind them as they exited.

He couldn't comprehend why Doctor Adams had a top-secret facility and why he was resuming his care. He felt he was making progress under Doctor Slocum.

CHAPTER TWENTY-ONE

MATTHEW SAT STUNNED IN his holding cell. The stench of urine emanated off of him. He couldn't understand how he had gotten himself into this mess. The police arrested him after they had tased him because he refused to drop the AR-15 he was holding. He put his head in his hands and tried to remember how he got the gun, and most importantly, why he had it. Matthew kept drawing a blank. They would hold his arraignment in the morning. For tonight, this holding cell was his home. They had interrogated him for hours, finally giving up. Exhaustion filled his body, however, sleep eluded him. Footsteps echoed in the hall leading to his cell. Two men in black suits accompanied a police officer.

"Looks like the feds are taking custody of you, kid, until your arraignment in the morning."

The officer opened up the holding cell and placed cuffs on Matthew. Then he turned him over to the two other men. The men thanked the officer and escorted Matthew into a black van waiting in the parking lot. As they buckled Matthew to the seat and closed the doors, one man said to the other.

"That was easier than expected."

"Sure was. The boss will be happy. Let's get this cargo to the airfield so we can get him to the boss."

Matthew couldn't understand why he would need to go to an airfield. Nothing that had happened in the last twelve hours had made sense. This was no different. He took slow, calming breaths, trying to keep his anxiety in check. It was late at night and dark inside the van, but he squinted his eyes to focus on the bench across from him. That was one thing. Then he struggled to clasp his hands together. That was two things. He needed three more things to help ground himself in reality so he wouldn't have a full-blown panic attack. Tapping his feet was the third thing. He couldn't think of two more things, but the breathing was helping.

Staying calm was important. He didn't have a good feeling about these men, and he doubted they were with the feds. If he could get away from them, maybe he had a chance. With handcuffs, there was no way he could run fast enough with his hands behind his back.

It was surprising how quickly they made it to the airfield. When the men opened the door to the back of the van, Matthew realized that their version of an airfield was nothing more than a wide-open field. It looked like a private landing strip. There was a small plane waiting apparently for them.

The men roughly extracted him from the back of the vehicle. Matthew had no chance of escape. He accepted his fate. They loaded him onto the plane and the pilot took off. It was really hard to keep his anxiety at bay. He was terrified of flying and the little plane they were on amplified that fear. He closed his eyes and soon fell asleep.

It was the bumpy landing at another private airstrip that finally woke Matthew up. He did not know where he was or how long they had been flying. When they climbed out of the airplane, there was another black van awaiting them.

The men shoved him into the van and this time didn't bother to buckle him in. Wherever they were going wound up being a brief ride because it felt as if they only drove for about ten minutes. When the door opened to the van again, Matthew realized they were in a cavern.

A man in a grey pinstriped suit greeted them. He was very familiar, although he had never seen the man in person. It was always through a computer screen, so he couldn't be sure it was the same guy.

"Welcome, Matthew. Please don't be afraid, we rescued you. They were planning on charging you with attempted murder and they were going to call for the most severe sentence. You are safe here under my care again. My colleagues will take you to where you can get cleaned up and put on new clothes. Then they will take you to your room."

Matthew didn't know what to think or feel. None of it felt right, though. Why did the doctor kidnap him from the police? His escorts did exactly what Doctor Adams had stated. His room had a cot, a toilet, and a sink. They closed the door and locked it as they left. He didn't know what was worse, the thought of jail or this place.

CHAPTER TWENTY-TWO

SPECIAL AGENT NUNEZ LISTENED intently to the news break. What were the odds that an anonymous tip thwarted another mass shooting? This wasn't adding up. The psychiatrist in Gabriel's case had made it sound as if he was the caller. He needed to analyze the calls. He knew the FBI recorded all the incoming calls. Picking up the phone, he dialed the number of his friend in New Jersey.

"Hey Mike, it's Nunez."

"Hey, what do I owe the pleasure of hearing from you? Miss me already?"

"Yeah, I miss you like the clap, Mike. Your visit was brief. That case you were working on out here wrapped up?"

"You are still the ray of sunshine, aren't you, Nunez? Yes, the case wrapped up quickly out there. Quicker than I had expected. So what do you need? You only call if you need help in a case. That seems to be constant with you. How did you ever pass training? Oh, that's right, you had me."

"Yah, yah, I owe everything to you. Anyway, you know that kid you guys just arrested? The one who was planning the mass shooting?"

"Yeah, we got a lucky break on that. We had a tip. I am glad we followed up on it. You know how that goes. So many are false."

"Definitely got lucky. We had a similar situation here about a month ago. The kid pleaded guilty to insanity and got a plea deal. The doctor testified he felt the kid called on himself. But now with your case happening, I question that. Do you think you can send me a copy of the recording of the tipster? I want to compare it to our unnamed caller."

"Hey yeah, I remember. I sat in on the pre-trial hearing when I was there visiting. You know, I didn't even think about any connection to your case. Probably just the flood of adrenaline from dealing with catching this kid. I will send you our recording. Can you send us yours? It might help to have more than one set of ears analyzing the recordings."

"Absolutely. I will send it via email tonight. Thanks."

"No problem. I am sending ours now. Hopefully, we can figure this out."

Agent Nunez hung up the phone. Within minutes, he received Mike's email and the other recording. He started listening to both, taking turns back and forth. The voices sounded the same to him. He would take it to the lab in the morning and have them run it through the voice analyzer.

Most of the night, his sleep was restless. Thinking about the similarities in the two cases. His buddy Mike had discussed some details of the case in his email. Both suspects had no recollection of their actions. They both destroyed their computers and cell phones as well.

Having the perpetrators in custody was so new to them all. Most mass shooters either wound up dead from the authorities trying to stop them or they killed themselves. The ones they could apprehend usually were stopped by armed citizens lately.

These two cases gave them a unique opportunity to study the motives behind these situations. Or at least try to. He thought after dropping off the voice files to the lab, he would pay a visit to Gabriel and interview him again. It was possible the doctor had made some progress, and he had regained his memories. He could only hope.

Morning came fast and Agent Nunez struggled to get himself motivated. When he looked in the mirror, the stubble on his chin showed signs of grey and his eyes had dark circles forming underneath. The hot shower helped to invigorate and wake him up. After shaving, he looked much more presentable, even though the circles still showed slightly.

He filled his travel mug with coffee and added a splash of Bailey's to it. The added pick me up would help him through the day. When he got to the lab, everyone there was working diligently on different cases. He found the technician he needed to talk to about analyzing the two files, and then he left.

His next stop was to visit Gabriel. As he entered the building, and made it to the desk on the floor, they assigned Gabriel to be on. He noticed a flurry of activity. He recognized Doctor Slocum, who was in charge of Gabriel's care, looking extremely flustered and somewhat irate. The other person he recognized was Gabriel's mom. She was standing holding onto the desk, sobbing. The doctor recognized Agent Nunez and came at him.

"Where have they taken Gabriel? Why was he transferred from my care? These court documents make little sense. Mrs. Ingles came to see her son, and he was gone. No one notified her of this transfer or us in advance."

Agent Nunez put his hands up towards the doctor.

"Whoa! I do not know what you are talking about. I came to talk to Gabriel myself. Let me look at that paperwork."

The doctor handed him the paperwork. It all looked legit.

"Is there a conference room I can use to make some phone calls, doc? I want to get some answers for you."

"Sure. Follow me down the hall. Nurse Jackie, can you bring Mrs. Ingles to my office and get her something to drink?"

Agent Nunez followed the doctor into a conference room.

"Here, I hope you can get some answers. We were making progress. Gabriel was having some flashes of memory recall in his dreams. He was opening up and telling me about them. I was hoping his identities were merging."

"No offense, doc, but I don't think the kid has a separate identity. An unnamed source stopped another mass shooter. Preliminarily, the voices of the two callers sound the same."

"Are you trying to say that Gabriel fooled me?"

"I don't know what to think, doc, but there is more to this than we originally thought. That is one thing I know for sure. Especially with Gabriel missing."

"What do you mean, missing? He was just transferred, right?"

"Doc, I have never heard of a transfer like this, and my office should have been involved if it was legit. I need to make some phone calls to be sure, though."

"Right, I will leave you alone to do your job. What do I tell his mother?"

"Tell her we are doing everything possible to get him transferred back here. That is all we can do."

They left agent Nunez alone in the conference room. Everything about this case was out of the norm. His first phone call was to his buddy, Mike. He had a sinking suspicion in his gut. The other suspect was in danger as well.

The phone call with Mike was chaotic. As Agent Nunez had suspected, they transferred their suspect in the middle of the night to supposed federal agents. However, all indications were that they were actual imposters. After more phone calls, he found out they forged the paperwork. They had two escaped fugitives or were they kidnapped? There was no way of knowing how to classify them. Were they dealing with a cell of domestic terrorists?

One thing was for sure, these kids were part of something much bigger than they originally thought.

CHAPTER TWENTY-THREE

Deric couldn't believe he had been able to stop two mass shootings from occurring. He was glad he had Adeline to confide in. No one else would believe him, anyway.

In school, the hallways and classrooms were abuzz with the news of the second mass shooter being thwarted and arrested. It wasn't until he was in study hall that a breaking news text came over his phone.

The text stated that both recent mass shooting suspects had escaped authorities and were on the run. There was an APB out for them and rewards for any information leading to their apprehension. They warned not to approach them, since they might have weapons and be dangerous.

Deric finished reading the text and shot a look at Adeline. She had been reading her phone as well. Their eyes met. In an instant, Deric thought to himself.

This is crazy. No way Gabe would risk escaping.

To his surprise, Adeline answered his thoughts in his head.

Why am I hearing your thoughts? I agree, though, that Gabe wouldn't try to escape.

Deric's eyes stayed locked on Adeline's.

What is happening? Why can we read each other's thoughts?

I don't know. Try looking away and thinking about something.

Deric looked away and thought how creepy it was they could read each other's minds. Then he looked back into her eye.

Anything?

When you looked away, I didn't hear your thoughts, but now that you are looking into my eyes, I can hear you again.

They are beautiful.

What?

Your eyes.

Adeline blushed. The bell rang and their gaze broke. It was time to switch classes. Deric realized he was having potent feelings for Adeline. Staring into her eyes was hypnotizing. He would have to keep those feelings in check, though. He knew with Gabriel and Matthew missing, he could be in danger as well. The thought of putting her in danger twisted his stomach. He could never forgive himself if something happened to her.

They had a study hall together next. Mr. Goldberg was the teacher. He was strict and didn't allow any talking or cell phones. They put the cell phones in a holder at the front of the class. They also had assigned seats, and both Adeline and Deric sat away from each other. So talking telepathically would be impossible. It was okay, though. Deric needed some time to process this newfound ability. He couldn't quite understand all of it.

He used his chrome book to look up telepathy. There was no scientific proof it was real. But he knew what he and Adeline had experienced was very real. Deric was feeling his palms sweat and the unsettled feeling in his stomach that he got when his anxiety was about to go full tilt on him. He took some long breaths.

Could he just be hallucinating? He would have to verify the conversation with Adeline when they got home. There was no way they could discuss what happened on the bus. If someone overheard their conversation, ostracizing would occur.

When they stepped off the bus, it was Adeline who busted out with the questions first.

"Did we really read each other's minds today?"

"I am afraid so. It was pretty creepy. I looked up telepathy in the study hall. There is no scientific proof of it being real. But we both experienced it."

"Yeah. It is definitely creepy. First, we appear in a couple of dreams together, now we can talk to one another through our minds. What the heck is going on?"

"I feel like I am in an episode of Stranger Things."

"Definitely."

"I wish I knew how to control the dreams. Like, make one happen. I haven't talked to Gabe since that second dream. I am worried about him."

"Maybe there is a way."

"How?"

"Have you heard of astral traveling?"

"Astral what?"

"Astral traveling. I have been trying to do it for a while. When we were in the dream with Matthew, I believe it was what happened. I had set an intention to astral travel. However, I didn't set a specific location. Then I ended up in the same dream as you two."

"Woah, so you mean to tell me there may be a way for us to travel in our dreams to talk to Gabe?"

"Maybe? I just started learning about it recently. I thought it would be cool to try. There is a meditation I listen to when I attempt it. I will send it to you. If we both try to set our intentions to go wherever Gabe is, maybe it will work."

"It is worth a try. So if you make it to Gabe and I don't, try to find out where exactly he is and how he got there."

"Sounds like a plan. See you in my dreams, Deric."

Adeline smiled as she walked away from Deric, leaving him blushing with his mouth ajar.

CHAPTER TWENTY-FOUR

GABRIEL HADN'T SEEN DOCTOR Adams since they transported him to this new facility. The men in black suits brought him his meals and meds. They didn't really watch him take the meds, so it was easier to dispose of them down the toilet after they left.

He knew he wasn't safe here, but he didn't understand why they took him from the other institution and brought him here. Why now? Was it because he was having flashes of memories?

He lay in bed, counting the ceiling tiles until he drifted off to sleep. When he awakened, it startled him to find Deric and Adeline in his little room.

"What are you two doing here? How?"

"Gabe, we don't have time to explain. We don't know how long we have to be here. Deric and I astral traveled here. Basically, in our dreams. Where are we, though? They have an APB out for you and Matthew. But it seems they locked you up. Were you caught?"

"Um, they transported me here. The feds did, at least that is what I was told. I don't understand why there would be an APB out for me and Matthew if the feds have me. Do you think Matthew is here as well? And how is Adeline here, though?"

"Yeah, about that. I was aware while in that first dream. Then I was in the dream with Matthew. Deric and I go to the same school now. They transferred my dad, and we had to move. So Deric and I have become friends. We don't know if Matthew is here. If he is, we will find him."

"That is very weird, that we can communicate in our dreams and share these experiences."

"Yeah, tell us about it. But we can't sit here and talk too long. We need to figure out where you are so we can rescue you."

"Deric, why would you need to rescue me?"

"If the feds had you in custody, why would they have an APB out for you?"

"I guess you have a point."

"Adeline, we need to get out of this room. How do we do it? We need to figure out where we are."

"I think we just focus on getting out of the room. Maybe focus on entering the hallway?"

Deric and Adeline closed their eyes and focused on the hallway.

When they opened them, they were in front of another door. They looked at each other and, without saying a word, focused on passing into the other room. There Matthew was fast asleep. They popped back out of the room. Neither Gabriel nor Matthew had escaped. They were both in custody. Deric and Adeline focused on being outside the facility and found themselves outside an enormous door in a tunnel. The tunnel led to the outside, which was on the side of a mountain.

There was a dilapidated sign that read Mt. King and Mt. Queen mining. They looked at each other and the next thing they knew; they were waking up in their own beds. Deric googled the mine and found it was in Colorado. They would have a long way to travel to get there to help Gabriel and Matthew. He texted Adeline.

They are in Colorado.

I know I googled it too. Should we alert the authorities?

Adeline, how do we know who to trust? Gabe thought it was the feds that transported him.

So what are we going to do?

We aren't going to do anything. I am going to Colorado to rescue them. You are staying here.

The hell I am! You go, I go. If I don't go, I tell the authorities.

Okay, we leave tomorrow after school. My parents work late tomorrow and so do yours, right?

Yes. But how are we going to get to Colorado?

Bus at first. We may have to switch that up once they discover us missing.

Okay. We should plan on ditching our phones too, so they can't track us.

Good idea.

CHAPTER TWENTY-FIVE

AGENT NUNEZ STARED AT the results from the lab analysis of both tipster phone calls. It was an exact match. Now how were they to find who this kid was? He had a first name from what Gabriel had told his shrink. Deric. But they did not know where this kid was from. How could two kids from two different sides of the country know the same kid?

The only logical answer was online gaming. Then it hit him that Gabriel had destroyed his computer. He picked up the phone to call his buddy Mike. He didn't know all the details of the other case, but he currently had one question on his mind.

"Yes, Nunez. What do I owe the pleasure of another call from you?"

"Hey, Mike. Look, I just got the results back from the voice analysis. It's the same kid that tipped us off for both shooters."

"Wow. That's good news, but how do we find this kid? What is the connection between the three?"

"Exactly my thought process, as well. What are most teenage boys addicted to?"

"Video games."

"Precisely, but Gabriel didn't have regular video games. He had a PC he built with his father. That he destroyed the day he planned on shooting up his school. Although he was genuinely shocked and upset when we showed him the pictures of the destroyed computer."

"Huh, that's odd. Not sure if it's a coincidence or what, but Matthew destroyed his computer too. When we showed him pictures, it devastated him. He had no memory of doing that or getting the gun. He had no memory of planning to shoot up the movie theatre."

"I think that's the connection. The computers. Maybe they are a part of some domestic terrorist group that communicates through computers. That's why they destroyed them."

"Could be, but how come they have no memory? I know Matthew could have just been saying that because of the publicity surrounding Gabriel's case and his getting put in a mental institution instead of jail. He convinced the psychiatrist he had no memory, right?"

"The no memory thing is weird. The psychiatrist called it some special form of amnesia. Another question, Mike, was Matthew being treated for any mental illnesses?"

"Actually, yes, he was seeing a therapist for depression and anxiety. He just turned 18 six months ago and left the group home he was living in for foster kids."

"Was he on any medications? If so, what ones?"

"Yeah, he was. The file will have to be looked at. I don't know off the top of my head. I will email you the file. Maybe you can find any connections or similarities. Right now, the upper brass is demanding answers on how and why he is missing. The public doesn't understand what happened. How can we even tell them these kids seem to have disappeared?"

"I understand. Heads are rolling here too. Thanks for the help."

"No problem."

So both boys were heavily involved in online gaming. Both suffered from depression and anxiety and were on medications. He would have to ask Doctor Slocum if the medications had side effects that might cause amnesia. This was definitely turning out to be a complicated case.

PART THREE

"ALL MEN OF ACTION are dreamers."
~ James Huneker

CHAPTER TWENTY-SIX

MITCH WAS FUMING. HE paced back and forth. The feds issued an APB for both kids. Gabriel's mom was on all the news outlets saying someone kidnapped her son. That he had not escaped. This had turned into an utter catastrophe.

He wanted to sit down with both boys and interview them, but he hadn't had a chance. The phone rang off the hook for hours straight. Members of his project wanted out. It scared them they were going to be found out and caught. None of them wanted to go back to prison. He guessed that's what he got for hiring former con men.

The clients, though, are what worried him the most. They were fearful of the repercussions and were demanding something be done with the boys.

Rubbing his hand over his chin, Mitch thought hard to come up with a viable solution to get himself out of the predicament. He knew his life was on the line. He walked over to his desk and opened the top drawer. His passport was sitting there. He could leave the country. There were plenty of places he could hide.

First, he must tie up all the loose ends, though. The boys would have to be disposed of. The bodies would have to be found close to where they disappeared from. Keep the authorities off his trail. He decided and then got to work rounding up the right people for the job at hand. Mitch had contacted his minion to get the ball rolling. It was a waiting game on his end.

As he sat in his chair, drumming his fingers on his desk, his phone rang.

"Hello, this is Mitch."

"Hey boss, I got two teams assembled. What do you want them to do?"

"Meet them at the cavern tomorrow. We will have to devise a foolproof plan so none of us gets caught. I will conference call you and share my thoughts when you are all there. Have them have their passports ready to leave the country as soon as the missions are complete."

"Okay, boss. Will do."

As Mitch hung up, he got another call. He recognized the number on the caller id. Hesitantly, he answered it.

"Hello."

"Hello yourself, Mitch. You have caused quite a commotion, haven't you? I thought you said you would have this handled?"

"I thought you said I had a month to handle it?"

"I did, however, you seem to make things worse."

"I will have matters handled by the end of the week, sir. I promise."

"A week then. No longer. We can't afford any more screw-ups by you."

Again, silence filled the other end of the phone. The bastard hung up on him again. He had to take care of the boys and leave the country. He knew he was a dead man walking.

In his bedroom, he got his suitcases out and started packing the necessities. He knew he could buy things where he was going. That offshore account he had was going to come in pretty handy. There was no way he could take his possessions with him. They would have to be destroyed.

Once he finished packing, he loaded his stuff into his pickup truck. Then he went to the shed and got a couple of containers of gasoline. He poured the gas as he walked through the home he had lived in for the last thirty years. He had just paid off the mortgage. It was bittersweet. His wife had left him twenty-five years ago. Right around the time, he started the program. She hadn't known what he was up to, but if she had, she wouldn't have approved, anyway. The money he made still paid for her lifestyle choices. There were no complaints from her about that.

As he walked out of the house for the last time, he lit a match and threw it onto the gasoline. The trail lit up as it raced through the house. He knew he only had minutes before someone would notice the flames and call the fire department. Driving down the driveway, he saw the flames consume the house in the rearview mirror.

There was no turning back now. It took him several hours to reach his destination. By the time he did, he committed to the idea that the kids would need to be killed. He needed information from them first. Who did they tell of their plans? He would have his teams employ their skills to extract the information.

CHAPTER TWENTY-SEVEN

DERIC HAD PACKED A **backpack with clothes** the night before. He stuffed it into his closet so he could just grab it when he got home from school. He was mad that Adeline had insisted on going with him, but he couldn't tell her no.

His mom drove him to school like always. He felt guilty knowing she would be upset coming home and finding him missing. It would break her heart. This almost gave him second thoughts. The thought of Gabriel and Matthew in that facility in Colorado and the nagging feeling they were in grave danger pushed away his guilt. As he got out of the car, though, he paused.

"I love you, mom."

The sudden exclamation of affection surprised Mrs. Whitaker.

"I love you too, Deric. Have a good day."

"I will."

When he saw Adeline, she seemed a little melancholy herself. She locked eyes with him.

I feel guilty not leaving a note for my parents. They are going to be devastated.

I know, I feel guilty too, but there is no way they will let us go across the country looking for Gabe and Matthew.

I know. It just sucks.

Deric grabbed her hand and held it as they walked to class. Several classmates stared as they walked together, holding hands.

The day seemed to drag on, which only amplified their anxiety about the plans they had. By the time school was over, they both were questioning their scheme.

They got home, grabbed their bags, and rode their bikes to Hamilton Avenue, where they caught a Seat bus to New London. Once they were in New London, they caught a Greyhound bus that would take them to Colorado. That was their intention. Deric had enough cash for both of their tickets. They had a short thirty-minute wait before they boarded the bus. They calculated they would be on the road for at least an hour before their parents would get home and notice they were gone.

Once on the bus, Deric and Adeline sat in the very back, trying to keep out of sight of most passengers. They wanted to avoid as many questions as possible. They had packed some snacks, and they ate as the bus embarked on the first leg of their trip. It would take them three days to reach Colorado from Connecticut. They just hoped they had that much time.

It was seven o'clock when Mrs. Whitaker got home. The first inclination that something wasn't right was that the house was dark. Usually, Deric had every light on when she got home. She hurriedly parked her car with a sinking feeling in her stomach. When she unlocked the door, Lexie, who was frantically wagging her tail and whimpering, met her. She let the dog out and then turned the lights on as she searched for Deric.

"Deric? Are you home?"

The quiet of the house sent shivers down her spine. She checked her *Find My Phone* app. His phone pinged at the same location as hers. If he was home, why wasn't he answering her? She checked his room. He wasn't there, but his cell phone was. There it was, sitting on his desk.

She heard George and Thomas coming in the door with their father.

"Deric is missing!"

Her husband stopped in his tracks and her other two sons got really quiet.

"What do you mean, he is missing?"

"I came home, and the house was pitch dark. His phone is here, but he isn't."

"Are you sure he isn't at Adeline's house? You know they have been spending a lot of time together."

"I didn't think of that. I am sure you are right."

Mrs. Whitaker dialed Adeline's parents. Her husband watched as she talked on the phone. His wife's face went pale, and she sat down on the couch, holding her hand to her mouth. Shaking, she was having a hard time holding back the tears.

"Adeline is gone, too. Her phone is in her bedroom. They are calling the police and suggest we do, too."

"You don't think they ran away or something, do you?"

"I don't know. Adeline's parents are distraught."

"Okay, I will call the police."

When the police arrived, they took as much information as the Whitakers could provide. They put out a silver alert. The police thought that the two teenagers had run away together.

It would be hard to convince Mrs. Whitaker they did, though. However, she kept thinking about how Deric had told her he loved her that morning when she dropped him off at school.

CHAPTER TWENTY-EIGHT

AGENT NUNEZ HAD MADE an appointment to talk to Doctor Slocum. When he arrived at the clinic, the doctor was very welcoming.

"Do you have any news regarding Gabriel and his whereabouts?"

"No, unfortunately, we do not. I have some questions for you, though."

"Of course, we can go to my office. I will do what I can to answer them."

The two men went into the doctor's office and sat down.

"What medications was Gabriel tak-ing?"

"He was on an antidepressant? Why do you ask?"

"Well, I am sure you are aware of the other kid that was arrested on the east coast for wanting to shoot up a movie theatre."

"Yes, thank god they stopped him just as Gabriel was."

"Well, we caught them both because an informant came forward to tell us they were going to commit the crime before it occurred."

"Yes, I know. As I stated in court, I be-lieve Gabriel suffered an identity crisis because of psychosis. Because of this, I believe he called on himself."

"Well, Doc, you are dead wrong. We analyzed the phone calls in both in-stances. It's the same kid, and it's not Gabriel."

"You say that some kid knew about both shootings before they hap-pened?"

"Yes, which means both Gabriel and Matthew were aware of their plans ahead of time and had to have shared those plans with this other kid some-how. Didn't you say his name was De-ric?"

"That's what Gabriel said he had dreamed his name was. None of this makes sense, though."

"Well, both boys were on antidepres-sants, and both boys were heavily into online gaming. My guess is they were friends online with this other kid and they somehow conspired together to commit these crimes. I don't under-stand how both of them supposedly can't remember anything, though."

"Agent Nunez. Gabriel's memory loss is real, I assure you. I couldn't access his memories through hypnosis. I attempted frequently. However, he said recently he had a few small dreams of him smashing his computer with a hammer, but he couldn't remember doing that when he woke up or under hypnosis."

"Doc, could the antidepressants cause loss of memory?"

"There is always that possibility we never truly know all the side effects of any medication, but the fact that Gabriel had no recall under hypnosis means that it goes deeper than just a medication side effect. Do you know if either boy was undergoing hypnotherapy with their prior therapists? I have heard of some adverse effects from the combination of hypnotherapy and antidepressants."

"I can find out. What kind of adverse effects?"

"Well, psychosis occurred in a small cohort during a study being done. They pulled the plug on the study, though. Most clinicians use one or the other, they don't combine them."

"Thank you, Doc. You have given me a lot of information and some leads as to what to look for next. Oh, who was the scientist in charge of that study? I may want to reach out to him."

"If memory serves me, it was Doctor Adam Mitchell. You are welcome. I just hope you find both boys safe."

Agent Nunez left the mental institution and headed straight to Gabriel's old doctor's office. The therapist was on the top floor of a medical building. When he got to the office, it surprised him to find the door to the suite locked. There was a note on the door stating that the office was closed for a personal emergency. There was another number to call if any patients needed help. He dialed the number.

"Doctor Jenning's office, Melissa speaking. How may I help you?"

"Hello, my name is Special Agent Nunez, with the FBI. I am standing outside Dr. Adams' office. Do you know where I can find him? I need to speak to him about one of his patients."

"I am sorry. He is missing at the moment. Our office is taking over his caseload until they find him."

"What do you mean, he is missing?"

"Well, sir. There was a fire at his residence last night. The place completely burned to the ground. They haven't found his body, but he is not answering his cell phone either. The police did a trace and came up with nothing. There is an ongoing search for his vehicle. That's all I know. Maybe the FBI can help find him?"

"Ma'am, do you have access to his files by chance?"

"No, sir. I imagine you would need a warrant for those considering patient confidentiality and all that."

"Okay, thank you very much for all of your help."

"I hope the FBI can help find him. We truly hope he is okay."

"Oh, one more question. Do you know if he practiced hypnotherapy on his patients?"

"As a matter of fact, he did. That was the only type of therapy he did."

"Thank you."

"You are welcome."

He had a bad feeling about Doctor Adams and his mysterious disappearance. He called Mike to check who Matthew's therapist had been.

"Hey Nunez, you are calling again? What do you need this time?"

"Yah, yah, I know. Are you even working on your case? Or are you letting me do all the work and you are going to take the credit, as usual?"

"Oof, low blow there, mate. I am working on it. Just from a different angle than you. I am trying to track down where my perp got the guns. So, what do you need now?"

"And what have you got chasing that angle?"

"Honestly, not much. Typical illegal gun with the serial numbers filed off. Most likely from a gang or illegal gun seller."

"Same here in our case. So there is another similarity. Anyway, I am chasing another angle, lead, whatever you want to call it. It still bothers me that neither of these kids remembers why they were going to commit these crimes. Or where they got the guns."

"They could be lying about their lost memories."

"Not Gabriel. Doctor Slocum is pretty adamant that Gabriel's amnesia is real. So I was wondering, who was Matthew's psychiatrist?"

"Isn't it in the file I sent you?"

"No, there is no name. Just that he was seeing someone and took medications."

"Hmm, I will look into that and get back to you, okay?"

"Sure, thanks."

It took about an hour for Mike to get back to Agent Nunez. The information confirmed his suspicions. Matthew had been seeing Doctor Adams through teleconferences. Now he felt he had enough probable cause to secure a warrant to get the records of both Gabriel and Matthew.

It took a couple of hours for the warrant to be secured. He met the deputies at the therapist's office. They had to break down the door to gain access. What they found inside was chaos. There were file cabinets left open and scattered papers on the floor.

To Agent Nunez, it looked like there had been some type of struggle. There were a few items knocked over from the desk and off the bookshelves. No sign of blood, though. No sign of forced entry anywhere. Was it a staged look to make it appear there had been a struggle? This doctor's disappearance became more suspect as the minutes ticked by.

After the team took pictures of how they found the office, they gathered the files and papers to bring back to Agent Nunez's office. It was late in the evening when Nunez pored over the files. There was no file on Gabriel or Matthew that he could find.

What he saw, though, was a pattern in the files. The good doctor saw an array of patients, male and female. However, he referred all the patients in the files he had to other therapists. The reason noted was that the patients he referred were not responding to his hypnotherapy techniques. He felt he could not help those patients. Oddly, though, agent Nunez could not find a single file on any patient that he was using hypnotherapy on. It seemed those files were missing. This led to more questions. He now had two missing suspects and the doctor of them both was missing. This case was becoming bigger than he first thought. And he still had no leads on who the unnamed informant was.

CHAPTER TWENTY-NINE

ADELINE'S HEAD WAS RESTING on Deric's shoulder as he leaned against the window. The bus was approaching the first stop where they would need to transfer to another bus. Deric's palms were getting sweaty. He knew by now their parents would know they were missing. How far they would look for them was the big question.

Deric gently woke Adeline from her slumber.

"Hey, we are going to be transferring buses soon. We should probably put our beanies on and put our hoods up, so our hair isn't showing."

"Okay, I am scared Deric. Our parents are probably worried sick."

"I know, I feel guilty too. But think about Gabe and Matthew."

"I know, I know. It doesn't make me feel any better."

They prepared for the transfer and followed other passengers off the bus. They looked to the board to see where their connecting bus was and moved towards it. There were TV screens throughout the bus terminal. One flashed a silver alert with their pictures on it. Deric and Adeline both saw it and looked at each other.

What do we do?

Act normal. Just keep walking towards the bus terminal.

They broke eye contact and continued on their way. Deric grabbed Adeline's hand when they saw a police officer walking towards them. She squeezed it back. As the officer got closer, Deric's heart raced and his pace slowed. When the officer was almost in front of them, Deric turned to face Adeline. He took her face in his hands and gently kissed her. Adeline's first reaction was utter shock. Then she melted into the warmth of his lips on hers. Deric watched as the police officer went right past them and he broke the lock he had on her lips.

Adeline stared into his eyes.

What was that for?

Umm, I had to make sure the police officer didn't recognize our faces!

That was quick thinking.

Thanks.

I am okay if we have to hide our faces again, just so you know.

Deric blushed and broke eye contact. Adeline smiled. They made it to the next bus and boarded it with no incident. Similar encounters filled the next few days. They made it all the way to Colorado without being intercepted by authorities.

They just hoped they had made it in time to save Gabriel and Matthew. The last leg of their journey was the most difficult. They hitchhiked to Mt. King and Mt. Queen. The road leading to the mine was snow-covered and treacherous. So they wound up walking the distance to the entrance to the cavern.

It didn't seem as if anyone was there. No guards were at the door. When Deric turned the knob, it surprised him to find it was unlocked. This made him nervous. He knew Gabriel and

Matthew were captives in their rooms. Having this front door left unlocked seemed out of sync with that knowledge.

Deric and Adeline slowly opened the door and entered the tunnel that led to the cavern. They knew where they needed to go because they had been there when they astral traveled. The difference was they knew they would encounter locked doors and people, eventually.

They carefully made their way to the sealed entrance of the cavern. A keypad locked it. They didn't know the code and they couldn't wait to see if anyone opened either the small door or the big garage-type door.

There were some crates stacked against the wall of the tunnel, and at the top was a vent. This gave Deric an idea. He communicated the idea to

Adeline, and they both started climbing. Deric was glad he brought his Leatherman because it had a screwdriver head he used to get the cover off the vent. Adeline had a pocket flashlight, so she crawled in first. She could see that the ductwork split up ahead, so she told Deric to climb in as well.

Once they were in, they went to the split. Deric turned himself around and went back to secure the vent cover so no one would see they tampered with it. Then he went back to Adeline. Instead of splitting up, they stayed together. They assumed the people holding Gabriel and Matthew were dangerous.

They came to a wider portion of ductwork and followed it until it came to another vent covering. As they peered out, they saw it led to the enormous cavern where there were vehicles parked. Two black vans were there with the doors to the cargo area wide open. There were two groups of men dressed all in black suits.

It was hard to hear what was being said between them, but a few key-words made Deric and Adeline meet eyes.

Did I just hear them say kill the boys?

Yes, I heard that too.

That means they are still alive for now.

How are we going to rescue them?

I don't know. We need to find them fast.

They backed their way through the ductwork to the last split. Deric tried to imagine where they were in comparison to their friend's rooms. He went left and followed the ductwork in that direction. Soon they came to another vent. It was Matthew's room. He was sitting on his cot with his head in his hands. Deric had never talked to Matthew other than in that original dream, so he didn't know how he would react to them trying to rescue him. He had to try.

"Pst! Hey Matthew. I know you don't know us. We are friends though. The guys that are holding you plan on killing you. We came to rescue you."

Matthew raised his head and looked around his empty room.

"Great, I am officially going crazy because I am hearing voices."

"I assure you. You are not crazy. We are up here in the vent."

"Who are you, and how do you know my name?"

"I am Deric, and my friend Adeline is here, too. Um, this is gonna sound strange, but we met you in a dream. The one where you killed everyone in the theatre."

"Holy cow! I remember that dream. I had it the day before they arrested me."

"Yes, sorry about that. I told the authorities."

"So I am here because you told, but people lived because they caught me?"

"Yes."

"Thank you. I didn't want to kill anyone. That dream was terrifying. It kept recurring for weeks! The one with you in it deviated from the norm. I remember nothing, though."

"Neither did Gabriel. We are here to save both of you."

"Who is Gabriel?"

"He was another kid who was going to commit a mass shooting. I dreamed about it and told the authorities. You are both being held here. But they are planning on killing you both. Can you reach up to this vent?"

"I think it's too high, even if I stand on my cot."

"We will be back. We need to find Gabriel and figure out how to get you both out of here."

"Okay. I will be here. Not like I can go anywhere."

Deric and Adeline crawled further and found another vent. This one was to Gabriel's room. They watched in terror as the men in black suits roughly grabbed Gabriel and put handcuffs on him.

"Today is your lucky day, kid. You are getting out of here for good."

"Am I going home? Will I see my mom and my sisters?"

The men just laughed as they pushed him into the hallway and the door slammed behind them.

Deric and Adeline crawled fast back to Matthew's vent and saw him being herded into the hallway by more men in black suits. They made it to the cavern vent just in time to see both of them shoved into the black vans.

As the big garage doors opened and the vans headed towards the opening, everyone and everything stopped abruptly. Swarms of FBI agents with guns drawn came in and started arresting everyone in sight. Deric and Adeline watched the scene unfold from the vent. It took a while for all the perpetrators to be caught and tracked down within the cavernous facility. When they were all in handcuffs, the FBI agent who seemed in charge rubbed his temples. He approached the group of men in black suits.

"Where are they?"

"Where are who? You have the boys in custody right there. Can you not see that?"

"I am not talking about them. Where are Deric and Adeline?"

Deric and Adeline froze. How did this guy know they were there? They had been so careful.

"Who is Deric and Adeline? We do not know who they are."

"They are two teenagers who disappeared from Connecticut three days ago. We have been tracking them across the country. One of our agents slipped an air tag on each of their backpacks at one of the bus stations. It couldn't be a coincidence that the kid Gabriel said he dreamed was the informant and the name of one of the kids missing was Deric. We knew they had to be connected. Then the girl was an old classmate of Gabriel's. We tracked them here. Our hunches paid off. They led us straight to you and the boys."

They knew. Deric felt defeated.

"We are here."

FBI agents quickly removed the vent covering and helped Deric and Adeline from the vent. Handcuffs went on Deric and Adeline's wrists. Then they stood next to Gabriel and Matthew.

"So you are Deric? My name is Agent Nunez. I hope you understand we are placing you in handcuffs until we determine your role in all of this."

"Yes, sir. I am Deric. Can you please let Adeline go? She does not know what is going on. She just came with me."

"No can do. She is an accomplice as you are, so we can not let either of you go."

Deric looked at Adeline and locked eyes with her.

I am so sorry; I got you involved in all this.

Don't be. I was involved as soon as I was aware within the dream. We are going to get through this.

CHAPTER THIRTY

AGENT NUNEZ ORDERED ALL the perpetrators to be transported back to the Colorado field office headquarters to sort it all out. It surprised him that his hunch panned out following the two runaways. It made little sense. However, nothing about this case was routine.

Doctor Adams was still missing. That was the last piece of this ever-complicated puzzle. He hoped the men they captured had clues to where he may have disappeared to. When they interrogated the prisoners, that would be the first question he would ask them all.

He believed all the teenagers were just innocent victims, but he couldn't be sure until he interviewed them all.

Deric, Adeline, Gabriel, and Matthew were all put in the same vehicle to be transported to headquarters. Agent Nunez insisted on driving them himself. He wanted to make sure they stayed safe. It astonished him his buddy Mike came all the way out to Colorado himself to be a part of this operative.

"Hey Nunez, I will drive this transport vehicle back to headquarters and make sure this scum gets there."

"Sounds good Mike, I will catch you back at headquarters."

As Agent Nunez drove off and out of the cavernous tunnel, it snowed.

Mike hopped into the driver's seat of the other transport vehicle. He knew what he had to do. The men were a liability that needed to be eliminated. He smiled as he realized the snow made his plan even more plausible. Traveling down the mountain was treacherous normally. In a snowstorm, it could be downright deadly. The rest of the agents and vehicles had already left, along with Agent Nunez. He was the last vehicle to leave.

The bridge was coming up. Mike unbuckled his seatbelt and increased his speed. He turned the wheel towards the edge of the embankment as he approached the river. Grabbing the brick from the passenger seat next to him, he opened the door, placed the brick on the gas pedal, and rolled out of the vehicle in one swift movement.

He hit the pavement hard. Rolling over, he watched as the van he had been driving careened down the embankment and into the freezing river below. It took a few minutes for the vehicle to become submerged completely.

Mike searched his pocket for his cell phone. It cracked the screen from the impact against the pavement. He just hoped it still worked. To his dismay, he had no service. The irony of it all. He crawled to the edge of the road and found a stick to help steady himself while walking. He was hurting, his leg was most likely broken. This was not part of his plan, but it worked as long as they found and rescued him from the storm.

Agent Nunez made it back to headquarters with the kids. He had them each brought into a separate interrogation room. Before he spoke to them, he wanted to read the files they had grabbed from the mountain facility. He had the files brought to the conference room they had set up as his makeshift office. It fully engrossed him when another agent interrupted him.

"Sir, Agent Sanchez hasn't made it back with the other prisoners yet. He isn't answering the radio or his cell phone."

"Get a bunch of agents and go search for him. That storm was getting bad when we left. Hopefully, he made it down off the mountain."

An hour later, Agent Nunez received a call.

"Sir, we found Agent Sanchez. It seems there was an accident. We notified emergency services. He is on his way to the hospital. He was barely conscious when we found him."

"The prisoners? Where are they?"

"Sir, we are searching. We don't know where the vehicle is and the prisoners. Agent Sanchez is delirious from hypothermia and his injuries. All we can get from him is there was an accident."

"Okay, keep me updated. Those prisoners can not go free. They are more dangerous than we originally thought."

"We will, sir."

Agent Nunez hung up the phone and ran his hands over his face. What he had been reading from the files had his mind buzzing. This was much bigger than he had originally thought. So far, what he had gathered was that Doctor Adams was an alias for the disgraced psychiatrist, Adam Mitchell, who had been part of a study to see the uses of hypnotherapy in patients on anti-depressant drugs.

He had falsified the documents in the study, saying the results were inconclusive when, in fact, he had found that they could use the therapy on some individuals for complete mind control. The files documented many cases in which he had successfully used the subjects to carry out missions of mass destruction. Doctor Adams had intended to sell the program to the highest international bidder.

This had major implications and ramifications. Agent Nunez did not know if international or even members of his own government were involved already in this program. The idea was to build an army of sorts that, at a moment's notice, would activate with a text message. The text would have the trigger phrase that would start the hypnotically programmed brain. They programmed each soldier to self-destruct when their mission was complete. If they captured them alive, there was no way they would remember why they were doing the mission or who had programmed them. They used gaming room chats to increase the hypnosis.

In all the files, there was no mention of Deric or Adeline. He didn't know how they fit into the complete puzzle. There were files on the men involved in carrying out the program. Agent Nunez came to a file that made his palms sweat. As he read, he couldn't believe what was in the file. His phone rang, startling him out of his bewildered thoughts.

"Sir, we found the van with the prisoners."

"And are they all accounted for and secure?"

"Sir, from what we can tell, they are all dead."

"What? How?"

"It seems the van veered off the road right before the bridge, must have hit an icy patch. It plummeted into the river. Agent Sanchez must have jumped from the van to save himself. We can't recover the van yet or the bodies inside. Thermal imaging seems to show us we account for all bodies."

"Thank you. What hospital was Agent Sanchez taken to?"

"St. Francis, it was the closest one."

"Thank you. I am going over to see him now. Hopefully, get his statement of what happened."

"Okay, it is going to be a while here."

Agent Nunez grabbed the file he had been reading and headed out to the hospital. He needed answers from agent Sanchez.

CHAPTER THIRTY-ONE

MR. AND MRS. WHITAKER were on the first flight to Colorado after receiving a phone call from Agent Nunez. They had found Deric and Adeline. The Degroots were traveling with them. They had received a call from agent Nunez as well. None of them understood why Deric and Adeline had gone to Colorado. They also didn't understand that their children were being held as accomplices to the two potential mass shootings.

Mrs. Whitaker looked out the airplane window as they taxied down the run-way. How did her boy get caught up in this? She was so worried about him. She had to keep her husband's temper in check. He was furious with Deric for running away and now to hear he was being held by the feds for conspiracy to commit mass shootings, he just was beside himself. His face was beet red and his legs shook as he opened and closed his fists.

"You know this has to be some big mix-up. Deric would never want to hurt anyone."

"I don't know what to think anymore. I thought none of our sons would run away, but here we are, flying across the country because our youngest did just that. And to top it off, he involved poor Adeline."

Adeline's parents were sitting across the aisle. They were both just as upset as the Whitakers. It was Mr. Degroot that said something first.

"I am not convinced that your son involved Adeline, or Adeline might have involved your son."

"What makes you think that?"

"We moved from Long Beach right after the attempted school shooting. Adeline was a classmate of the first shooter. We moved to get away from all of it. Yet here we are, dragged back into it."

"You don't believe your daughter has anything to do with all this, though, do you?"

"I honestly don't know what to believe. I thought moving her across the country would keep her safe, yet here we are flying back to find out what trouble she has gotten herself into."

Neither Deric nor Adeline's parents could believe their children had anything to do with the mass shooters. It was all surreal. When their plane touched down in Colorado, they couldn't wait to get to FBI headquarters to see their children. Agent Nunez had sent a car and an agent to meet them.

The ride to headquarters was quiet. The agent escorted them to a conference room and gave them coffee while they awaited further instructions.

Down the hall in another conference room, Mrs. Ingles sat waiting to see her son Gabriel. She did not know what would happen next, only that they found her son and he was alive. She imagined they would transport him back to the institute to serve out the rest of his sentence. The question remained though who had kidnapped her son and why.

There were no parents for Matthew. He had been a ward of the state in the foster system. When he aged out, he turned to living on his own. Each of the teenagers sat alone in an interrogation room.

The trip across the country had exhausted Deric. He was so afraid of what his parents would say when they saw him next. Were his parents even aware of where he was? Surely, the feds had notified them. His thoughts went to Adeline. He hoped she was okay and she wouldn't get into too much trouble. He wished she had stayed home.

Adeline shivered in the room as she waited to be asked questions. She would do her best to hide Deric's dream powers and their telepathic bond. Who knows what they would do to them if they found out they had powers? Hopefully, Deric would keep the powers to himself as well.

Gabriel felt safe in Agent Nunez's care. He hated the wait to see his mom. He knew she had to have been worried sick about him.

Matthew was sweating profusely. He wiped the palms of his hands on his pants, even with them handcuffed together. Everything was still so confusing. He didn't understand why they were all at the FBI headquarters.

CHAPTER THIRTY-TWO

AGENT NUNEZ WALKED INTO St. Francis Hospital and up to Agent Sanchez's room. As he walked in, he saw his old friend Mike sitting up in his hospital bed. He looked a little beat up, but nothing a few days of rest and relaxation wouldn't cure.

They had gone through training together. In the past, they worked side by side until they both got assigned to separate field offices. They had stayed in touch. He rubbed his chin with his hand and dropped the file on Mike's hospital tray.

"Hey man, it's good to see you. What's this?"

Mike picked up the file and thumbed through it. His face went ashen.

"Man, it's not what it looks like. I was working undercover."

The beads of sweat rolled down the sides of his face. Agent Nunez slammed his fist onto the tray.

"Innocent kids, Mike. Used for what? Innocent people killed for research? Help me understand how this was allowed to proceed all these years. As soon as you knew his plans, you should have stopped him!"

"It's not that easy, bro. You need to let it go. Doctor Adams is gone. He disappeared. With him gone, they dismantle the program. His cronies are all gone. It ends, all of it. If you pursue this, your life will be in danger. I am risking everything to even tell you this."

"What are you saying? How do you know his cronies are all gone? Unless. You didn't do anything rash, did you?"

"I am not saying I did. What needed to happen, happened. You need to just close the case. "

"What about those kids? They are innocent pawns in all of this. We shouldn't allow their lives to be destroyed because of some experiment gone wrong."

"If you expose the program and let those kids go free, you are sealing their fate and yours."

"Is that a threat?"

"No. This is bigger than even you can imagine. Let it go, Nunez."

Agent Nunez picked up the file and walked out of the hospital. He sat in his car, pondering his next move. What he knew is those kids didn't deserve to have their lives destroyed. If what Mike said was true, that pursuing this case would lead to more trouble than it was worth, he didn't know what his next move should be.

If he told his superiors about this program and what it entailed, what would happen? Mike seemed to think it was the wrong move, but was Mike a bad guy or a good guy? After reading the file and talking to Mike, he didn't know. He hoped the drive back to headquarters would clear his mind.

As he approached the command center, he heard the roar of fire trucks and sirens. Pulling into the parking lot, he couldn't believe his eyes. The FBI base was on fire. He scrambled to get out of his car and find someone to tell him what was going on. He grabbed the nearest agent.

"What happened?"

"Someone detonated an incendiary device in the conference room you were using as your office."

"Was anyone hurt? Where are the prisoners?"

"The prisoners are secure. The parents are all safe. There seem to be no injuries, sir. The bad news is all the files you were working with are probably gone."

Agent Nunez ran both hands through his hair. This was what Mike was warning me about. People didn't want this information revealed. People who could get inside FBI headquarters and destroy evidence. Powerful entities. It made his skin crawl and his stomach turn. He got into this field to stop the injustices of the world, not to be a part of them.

As the firefighters worked to put out the fire, agent Nunez devised a plan of action swiftly. He was going to put Gabriel and his family in a witness protection program. It was the only way to make sure he stayed safe and could live out the rest of his life in freedom. The same for Matthew. Since there had been an APB out for the boys, he could manipulate the narrative with the press.

They will announce the boy's bodies found. He would help Mrs. Ingles with a fake funeral and then move her. It would make sense for her to move and start a fresh life after losing Gabriel. That is what she did when she lost her husband. Maybe she would share her new home with Matthew. It would be easier for him to keep tabs on both boys. With Doctor Adams still missing, he didn't know if they were in danger.

The only problem was Deric and Adeline. He still didn't know how they fit into this convoluted puzzle. They weren't part of the program that he knew. So he was the only one who had questions for them. He decided to interrogate each of them separately in his car. He gathered Deric first.

"Hey there son, I am sorry this has to be done this way, but as you can tell, things are chaotic at the moment. I want to get this over with so that I can reunite you with your parents."

"Okay, sir. Are my parents here?"

"Yes, they are here and they are safe. My first question for you is going to be straightforward. What were you doing at the cavern?"

"I was there to rescue Gabriel and Matthew."

"How did you know where they were?"

"I had a hunch because of a dream I had."

"Wait. You traveled halfway across the country based on a hunch from a dream?"

"Yes, sir."

"What made you believe your dream was accurate?"

"Well, sir, not that you would believe me, but it isn't the first time I have dreamed something and then it came true."

"So you are telling me you are psychic? You have dreams that come true?"

"Yes, sir. I guess you can say that."

"That's how you knew about the shootings before they happened?"

"Yes, sir. I was the one that called the authorities. May I say something else?"

"Well, thank you for tipping us off. I am sorry we arrested you. What do you want to add?"

"Adeline just came along for the ride. I told her I was going to look for Gabriel and Matthew, and she insisted on coming along. I told her not to."

"It's okay, son, I believe you. I am going to talk to her next. As long as your stories match up, I will reunite you with your parents and you will be free to go home."

Agent Nunez brought Deric back to where they had been holding him and Adeline in another transport vehicle. As they put Deric back in the van, he locked eyes with Adeline.

Just tell him you found out I was going to look for Gabriel and Matthew and you insisted on coming along. Understand?

Yes.

A short while later, Adeline returned uncuffed with Agent Nunez. He took Deric out of the van and uncuffed him. They were both reunited with their parents. Agent Nunez addressed the parents.

"Your children are free to go home with you all. There won't be any charges against them. They were just following online leads, and since Adeline was friends with Gabriel, they wanted to help find him."

Adeline locked eyes with Deric.

Why is he covering for us?

I don't know, but most likely to cover up the fact they tracked us to the bad guys. Our parents might not like that.

True. Any word on Gabriel and Matthew?

No. Should I ask?

Not in front of our parents.

Okay, I will try to get agent Nunez alone before we leave.

Deric's parents hugged him, and Adeline's parents did the same with her. There were scolds about running away and leaving the detective work to authorities. Agent Nunez personally escorted them to a hotel for the night personally. Before he left, Deric caught him alone.

"Agent Nunez, what about Gabriel and Matthew? Are they going to be okay?"

Agent Nunez struggled to tell Deric the truth. If his plan to keep Gabriel and Matthew safe was going to succeed, he had to lie.

"Sorry kid, they sustained fatal injuries in the blast back at headquarters."

Deric put his hands over his face. He fought back the tears.

"Thanks for letting me know. I tried so hard to save them and in the end, they died anyway. It just isn't right."

"I know, kid, it wasn't your fault. By turning them in, you saved countless lives, and that is something to be proud of. If you have any more dreams, call me directly. I will make sure we follow them up."

Agent Nunez handed Deric his card and then left.

CHAPTER THIRTY-THREE

GABRIEL WAS SITTING IN a transport van. They had put him in it after being evacuated from the building. These vans made him jumpy. They never led to anything good happening. When the back door opened and he saw his mom with Agent Nunez, he burst into tears. His mom climbed into the van and gave him a big hug. Then Agent Nunez climbed in and closed the doors.

"Gabriel, I don't have the authority to set you free, even though I believe you are an innocent pawn. I can't explain why I know this and I can't prove it because all the evidence has gone up in flames tonight. What I can do is offer you semi-freedom. I can conjure a narrative and place you in witness protection, giving you, your mom, your sisters, and Matthew new identities and a fresh start."

"How can you do that?"

"I have connections and ways. But I need you to decide right now if that's what you want. I will take you and Matthew to a safe house. Your mom will fly home and have a funeral for you. Then she and your sisters will meet up with you at the safe house."

"I have to die?"

"You won't really be dead, of course, but your old identity will be dead."

"I will be free to live my life, normally?"

"Yes, although I will check up on you and Matthew periodically to make sure you are staying out of trouble."

"The other kid?"

"Yes, your mother has agreed to take him in. You two have been through a lot and can hopefully help each other heal from it all."

"Okay, I agree, let's do this!"

Agent Nunez left Gabriel and his mom alone. He needed to go talk to Matthew and give him the same choice. Of course, when he talked to him, he was agreeable. Matthew was excited most about having a family to go home to.

It was well into the early morning hours when agent Nunez and the boys arrived at the safe house. They were all tired, and he showed the boys to their room. Gabriel and Matthew were both grateful for the comfortable beds. They were fast asleep as soon as their heads hit the pillow.

Even though Agent Nunez was exhausted from the previous evening, he had one more thing to do. He suspected he already knew the answer, but he wanted to hear it for himself.

"Hello, St. Francis Hospital, how may I direct your call?"

"Yes, can you connect me to the nurse's station on floor five, A wing?"

"Sure, sir, okay, please hold."

"Okay."

"Nurse's station A5. How can I help you?"

"Hi, I am calling to get an update on a patient. He is a friend of mine. Michael Sanchez. He is in room 514."

"I am sorry sir, your friend passed away around ten o'clock last night. He had a cardiac arrest."

"Thank you."

Just as he suspected. They took Mike out of the equation. Hopefully, Agent Nunez had taken the steps to ensure the kids, and himself were safe. He had only let his inner circle, those he most trusted, be involved with the plans for the boys. This made him feel secure they would all be safe. Before he closed his eyes, he sent out a press release to national media that they had apprehended the boys, however; they died in the explosion and fire at the headquarters they had held them at.

He did everything that needed to be done, including requesting the transfer to the closest field office to where he was going to be setting up the boys. He wanted to be close so he could keep an eye out. The people involved in the program were dangerous. He knew this. Hopefully, the news the boys were dead would put an end to the danger to them.

One could only hope.

CHAPTER THIRTY-FOUR

DERIC WALKED BACK TO the hotel rooms where his parents and Adeline's family were. He couldn't look at Adeline. His eyes were welling up as he tried to tell them about Gabriel and Matthew. When he completed what he was saying, Adeline burst into tears and ran to the bathroom, locking herself in it. Deric's parents ushered him into their room, leaving Adeline's parents to comfort her.

"I am sorry, son. I know Adeline is your friend, and she was friends with Gabriel. It's best we let her parents comfort her."

"Sure, dad."

There was no telling his parents the connection he had with Gabriel. They wouldn't believe him even if he tried. He climbed into bed and quietly cried himself to sleep. There would be no comfort for him until he could be alone with Adeline and talk through it all privately.

In the morning, his family met up with her family for breakfast. Adeline's eyes were puffy and bloodshot. It was obvious she had done a lot of crying. Her parents were doing everything to console her. They got her everything she normally loved from the breakfast buffet, but she just picked at her food and pushed it around her plate with her fork.

Deric was just as silent and picked at his plate as well. The parents did their best to keep the conversation light as they discussed their plans for flying home. Adeline broke into their conversation.

"Dad, can we go to Gabriel's funeral? Please? He was my friend, and he deserves to have his friends at his funeral."

Her father looked at her mother, who just shrugged and shook her head yes.

"I guess he deserves that. And you deserve the closure as well, sweetheart."

Deric looked at his parents. He didn't know what they would say, but he had to try.

"Can I go too? I want to be there for Adeline."

His mother looked at his father, whose patience seemed to wear thin.

"If it's okay with Adeline's parents, I think your father and I can agree to it. But, when you come back, we are grounding you for a month for pulling this running away stunt. You hear me?"

"Yes, mom, thank you. Dad, can I go? If they will take me?"

"Son, I understand you want to be there for Adeline. I am still pretty mad at you for running away. But, since you are asking and not just doing, and you have accepted your punishment, I will let you go. If her parents don't mind you going."

Adeline looked at her parents, pleading with her eyes to say yes.

"Well, you have been a good friend to Adeline and even went along on her adventure to find her friend. I guess you deserve some sort of closure your-self."

For the first time since they had heard the news of Gabriel's death, they both smiled. Instead of fly-ing home to Connecticut, Deric flew with Adeline's family to California for Gabriel's funeral in Long Beach. His parents had boarded a flight back home.

It was hot in California and Deric could not wait to get back home to the mild weather he was used to. He hadn't been to too many funerals be-fore. His parents had given him some money to buy some decent dress clothes to wear. When he went with Adeline's parents to the store to pick them out, he went with khaki shorts and a short sleeve button-down dress shirt. He wanted to be comfortable and cool.

The funeral was small. Very few people attended and there were even a few protestors holding signs saying Gabriel was now where he belonged. This angered Deric and made him sad. They didn't know Gabriel. Adeline saw Agent Nunez first and elbowed Deric, then locked eyes with him.

Why do you suppose he is here?

I don't know. Maybe to bring some comfort to Mrs. Ingles?

I suppose it just all seems weird and a bit off. The case is closed. There really is no need for him to be here.

Agent Nunez caught sight of Deric and Adeline and just gave them a nod in acknowledgment. As Gabriel's mother placed his ashes into the ground next to his father, she wept. His sisters clung to their mother, crying as well. Agent Nunez put his sunglasses on and walked back to his car.

They didn't stay long after the service was over. Adeline's parents had made dinner reservations with some old friends since they were in town. Deric and Adeline convinced them to let them stay back at the hotel suite they had been staying in. The kids ordered a pizza and just watched *Stranger Things*. They did not lose the irony of what they had endured over the last few months and what happened in the series.

The next day, they were on a flight back home. When they dropped Deric off at his house, he said thank you to Adeline's parents and then waited for his parents to get home from work. As he did, he dozed off.

When he awoke, he didn't recognize where he was. What he recognized

were Gabriel and Matthew sitting together on a couch, laughing. Was he
dreaming or was he dead, too?

"Am I in heaven with you two?"

The boys stared at him and laughed.
It was Gabriel who spoke first.

"Dude, it's good to see you! But no,
this is not heaven. This is a safe house
we are living in. We aren't dead, but
if you are here and talking to us, that
means we are all sleeping and dreaming. I still can't get used to this."

"How many times have you guys
done this?"

"A couple now. It's how Adeline and
I could find you, and ultimately, how
Agent Nunez found you and apparent-
ly saved you."

"Yeah, he said we were innocent
pawns, but they destroyed his proof in
the fire. So he set this up. He is giving
us new identities."

"I just attended your funeral yester-day Gabe, sorry Matthew, I don't know when or where yours was. Gabe, it dev-astated your mom and sisters."

"I am touched that you went. My mom and my sisters are joining us soon. They are moving to make a new life. Agent Nunez set it all up."

"No worries, man. They probably aren't even having a funeral for me. I didn't have a family before. Now I do. These dreams are weird. Have you all figured out how we can do this?"

"I am so glad you are both alive! Ade-line and I are thinking it's some sort of astral travel. We are going to research it more. You guys should too! Oh, and another freak thing we have figured out. When we lock eyes, we can read each other's minds. It is peculiar, but cool."

"No way! That is amazing. I wonder if we can do that? We will have to try when we wake up."

"No offense, bro, but I really don't want to lock eyes with another dude."

Deric and Gabriel laughed.

"Yeah, Deric gets the best eyes to look at. We can still try it and see if we have the same ability."

"I guess. Just don't kiss me!"

The boys laughed and then Deric woke up to his mom gently shaking his shoulder.

"Are you okay, Deric?"

"Mom, I am well, thanks. I am sorry for the trouble I caused. I love you."

"It's okay. I am just glad you are finally safe at home. I love you too."

The end.

RECOGNITIONS

Thank you to my Mom, who continues to be my number-one fan and supporter. I love you!

Thank you to my husband and my sons who listen to me ramble on about my writing, book covers, editing, formatting, promoting, and who understand when I am in "The Zone" and everything else gets blocked out. Love you all, even if you have read none of my books! You all support me in other ways and I appreciate that!

Thank you to my big brother Keith and his family for their support and encouragement. I love you all.

Thank you to my editor and friend Louise, who helps to polish my work and also sends me encouraging memes!

Thank you, R.K. for your amazing proofreading skills, for catching those minor errors that slip through, and for always encouraging me!

Thank you to D.H. my badass niece in Law Enforcement, who patiently and enthusiastically provided me with accurate information on what can occur when a subject is tased. Also, a shout out to her colleagues who also provided information through her. You all rock! Much love to you all!

Thank you to all of my aunts, uncles, and cousins who have read my books and recommended them to others! I love you all and appreciate all the support.

Thank you, Raven, Dawn, Christina, Laura, Brittany, and all the other outstanding administrators of the various Facebook book groups that welcome authors and allow us to promote in their groups. You help us authors so much, and this author appreciates it! Keep slaying those books, book dragons!

Thank you to my ARC readers for this book. Lynn, Michaeleen, Ella, Dawn, MariAnna, Carina, Angie, Cassie, Kathy, Jo Di, Karen, Raven, Sue, Dennis, Lauren, and Kylie.

About Author

A former paraeducator, novice genealogist, turned author D.M. Foley is an award-winning writer. Her first book, The Lyons Garden Book One Family Ties, received The New York Best Sellers Gold Award in December 2021. She lives in Southeastern, Ct, with her husband, three sons, and her mom.

You can follow her on her social media accounts at:

D.M. Foley - Author Page on Facebook
@d.m._foley on Instagram and TikTok
@DMFoleyauthor on Twitter
Contact Information:

d.m.foleyauthor@gmail.com
D.M. Foley
P.O. Box 735
54 Main Street
Jewett City, CT
06351

BOOKS IN THIS SERIES

Deric Dream Changer Book1 Of The Dream Walker Series

BOOKS BY THIS AUTHOR

The Lyons Garden Book One Family
Ties
Erasing Secrets The Lyons Garden
Book Two
Pawns The Lyons Garden Book Three

Deric Dream Changer Book 1 Of The
Dream Walker Series